Splitting Souls

Kaylynn Hunt

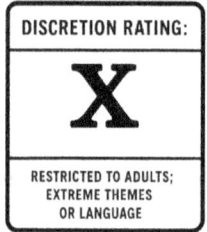

DISCRETION RATING:

X

RESTRICTED TO ADULTS;
EXTREME THEMES
OR LANGUAGE

Chapter 1

Gideon

Whelp, there goes my lunch. I just walked out of the most gruesome crime scene I've ever seen. The flashes of what I'd just witnessed wouldn't leave my head. There was no point in trying to forget now; I had to go back in there. I took a few more deep breaths of fresh air. Hopelessly wishing I could fill my lungs enough that I wouldn't have to relive the stench of that room.

The victim's clothes were neatly folded atop the moderate dresser. Her purse, with identification, was placed next to the clothing. There was a pair of prescription eyeglasses next to the purse, along with a set of car keys, all lined neatly in a row. The victim's shoes were placed by the door, toe to the wall, perfectly aligned with one another.

I took in the scene; there didn't seem to be anything else out of place, with the exception of the corpse, of course.

1

Propped up in the bed was a young woman, possibly in her mid-twenties. She was nude; it appeared she'd been there a few days. She had a medium brown complexion and long hair that appeared to have been combed. Her eyes were open, and her legs were spread. And there, between her legs, the blood trail started. It ran from the center of her body to the bottom of her feet, where a fetus lay, still attached with its umbilical cord. It appeared to be full term or nearly. I could make out the features, gender, and hair on top of its head. Not sure if it ever took a breath.

I took my notes and got out of there as quickly as possible. Any other information to be gathered would have to come from the crime scene analyst's report. My focus turned to where this woman came from, how she got in that room, who had seen her last, and with whom. According to the driver's license in her wallet, Marissa Hannigan was from West Virginia, which was quite a way from this great state of Oklahoma.

"Were you here when the young woman checked in?"

"I wasn't here. I believe she must have come in the other night. Shirley runs the night shift. You'll have to check with her," the motel clerk answered.

"Ok. Had you seen anyone else go into that room, heard anything?"

"No, sir. Come to think of it, I don't think I ever saw the young lady. I did walk past her door the other morning and heard her talking. I didn't hear another voice; I assumed she was on the phone."

"Did you hear what she said?"

"Not really, sir, nothing I can recall anyway."

"Thank you. If you think of anything else, let me know," I told him as I handed him my card.

I didn't recall seeing a cellphone.

"One other thing, can you look at the records and see if that call was made from the motel phone?"

"Sure, one second."

The clerk clicked a few keys on the computer in front of him.

"No, it doesn't look like she used the in-house telephone."

"Thanks," I said as I walked back toward the scene of the crime, room 213.

It looks like word has already gotten around. The news vans had pulled up outside the parking lot entrance. We'd cordoned off the area. Well, the uniforms had. But I had no intention of getting sucked into the whirlwind of the media.

"Hey, George, keep a lookout for a cellphone."

"You got it," one of the crime scene techs responded.

One other thing that was missing was the victim's car, which was odd because her keys were there on the dresser. When I pressed the remote to locate it in the parking lot, nothing happened. I made my way to the office to do my research on the vic. I'd gotten all I needed and seen more than I wanted.

Once I settled in at my desk, it only took a few minutes to gather the initial information I needed. It appeared that Marissa Hannigan was not married. Whatever vehicle she was driving wasn't registered to her. No one had reported her missing yet. She attended Langston University, which explains why she was in Oklahoma but not why she was in a motel room outside of Lawton. Marissa was twenty-three years of age when she took her last breath.

To make sure all the bases were covered, I jotted down all the things I wished to learn about Marissa. When was the last time anyone had seen or spoken to her? Who was she dating? Did she have friends? Where did she work? Who did she have listed as an emergency contact?

I'd be taking a trip to the school in the morning.

This was my routine, a ritual almost. The list served as a point of reference so that I didn't forget anything. More importantly, it allowed me to unload before I went home, you know leaving the job at the job. A few other things made the list and I headed home.

The next morning started early for me. I was at Langston's administrative office before their doors even opened. I'd done quite a bit of brainstorming and hypothesizing on the two-plus-hour drive from Lawton to Langston. There still hadn't been a missing person's report. Most certainly, I had to work out a notification for her parents. We needed to find out how long she'd been at Langston. There were many things added to my list. My most pressing question currently was, where and who was the father of that baby?

After spending half the day at the college, I'd learned a little but mostly nothing. Because the parents hadn't been notified, I didn't want to let on that Marissa was no longer with us. As far as anyone at the school knew, we were just trying to determine her whereabouts. I talked to the counselor, her professors, her roommate, and neighbors. They all pretty much told the same story. Marissa was a quiet one. She kept to herself but wasn't unfriendly. She was a recipient of a prestigious academic scholarship. Marissa maintained more than her minimum requirements. But as of late, no one had seen much of her. No significant love interest was known by anyone. And apparently, she'd hidden her pregnancy well. It seemed to be a surprise to everyone.

As I headed back, I thought over all the conversations. There was one particular professor who stuck out for me; I'm not sure why. But something in my gut was telling me to look more into Dr. June Sumpter. Not sure if it's my cynical mind, however, she just seemed to be overly (something), can't pinpoint it. She was trying too hard to make me believe she didn't know much about the girl. I think she knew more than what she was saying.

The roommate was clueless, more self-centered than anything. The counselor pointed out that Marissa seemed a little less stressed the last time she'd seen her. I made a note to get an update on some of the other records I'd requested. Her bank statements and cellphone records were the most pressing.

My ringing phone interrupted my thoughts.

"Hey, sunshine."

"Hi, honey. Will you be home in time for dinner?" My wife asked.

"Yes. I'm headed back now. I should be pulling in in less than an hour."

"Can't wait, I cooked your favorite."

"Yum, I got something else I want to taste."

"Look at you being mannish. I'll see you in a few."

Once I disconnected the call, I changed my music to begin my ritual of ridding myself of the day's work. I didn't like to take all the negativity into the house. And I never talked about work with Serita. We've been married for three years now. I will never forget the day we met.

It was my first day of college. The first time I'd ever been away from home, I was completely overwhelmed. I was standing outside the common hall trying to figure out where I was supposed to go next. The sea of people in front of me seemed to part as if they were red and she was Moses. She was the most beautiful thing I'd seen in my life. Serita looked like an Egyptian goddess reborn. She walked right toward me, and I know I must've looked like I belonged in special ed classes because she offered her assistance.

"Can I help you find something?"

I couldn't even answer; I just pushed the schedule I had in my hand in her face.

"Oh, that's the third building right over there," she said, pointing in the direction I needed to go.

"Thank you," was all I managed.

Serita kept walking.

From that day forth no other woman existed to me. It took me nearly a month to work up the courage to speak to her. But I took the time to prepare. I wasn't ever one to beat around the bush. So, I didn't make any excuses or small gestures, I put on a grand show to ask her out on a date.

Chapter 2

IT HAD BEEN THREE weeks since Marissa's body was found, and I was no closer to what happened than on day one. We had visited the parents. I had the unfortunate notion that a sense of duty existed, requiring me to make the notification in person, myself. It wasn't a pleasant thing. But you'd imagine nothing of this magnitude would ever be pleasurable. I think the hardest part was having to inform them of the deceased grandchild, whom they seemed to know nothing about. I did get a sense of the kind of person Marissa may have been. That helped me to ask other questions.

The father of that baby had yet to make an appearance, which pressed at a nerve for me. What man wouldn't come looking for the mother of his soon-to-be child? Maybe they'd fought. Maybe she'd run away from him. Perhaps he never wanted the child. Had he done this? I was sure the answer to that last question was no. The person responsible put her on a display. That was for a reason.

There was some message in the manner in which Marissa was presented. But until I could figure out who or what else Marissa may or may not have involved herself with, I couldn't decipher what they were trying to say. With all that being said, this day sent me in a whole different direction. I needed medical records, information I could only gather at the behest of a judge's instruction. As such, I'd gotten permission from her parents to make the request. Not sure it would help sway the judge, but they were her next of kin, so fingers crossed.

"Hey, Robin, did we get anywhere on those phone records?"

"Still making my way through the list, Boss. I'm working my way backward. It seems whoever she spoke with last was on a burner."

"Keep me posted."

"Barton, you got another case?" the chief called from his office door. "Line two."

"I'm on it."

I groaned, then picked up the phone on my desk. After jotting down the address, I stood to head out.

Though I was knee deep in not knowing what happened to Marissa, there wasn't anything I would be able to do. It was a stalled case until I got something back from the judge or Robin turned something up.

When I arrived at the scene, behind a small neighborhood service station, I expected to see a gang banger laid out. The officer on the initial call told me we had a gunshot victim. Seeing one uniform out front in tears should've clued me in that it was far from a run-of-the-mill gang shooting. I rounded the corner of the building, putting on my gloves, and ducked under the tape. When I looked up, I nearly lost not only my lunch but my entire stomach.

Propped against the back wall of the market, nearly blocked by the commercial dumpster, was an amber-skinned woman. Her hair was cut in low natural curls, eyes open, gunshot wound to the forehead, where some say your third eye would be. This woman was clothed, unlike Marissa. But like Marissa, from her center to her feet, there was a trail of blood which led to a fetus still attached to its mother's lifeline.

My heart began to race. There were a multitude of reasons, but at the moment, I just needed to calm down. Pulling out my phone, I dialed Robin.

"Yeah, Boss."

"I need you to get off what you're doing right now. Find out if there has been any type of violence or murder of pregnant women or women and their newborn babies in other states, say, in the last five years."

"O...kay," she stated apprehensively.

I couldn't be bothered with saying anything else. The small crowd about ten feet away started to grow. I just disconnected as I began talking.

"Officer, push this crowd further back. Canvass anyone standing there, get their info. Find out if they saw anything. By all means, don't give any information, and for the love of everything holy, ignore all media."

"You got it, Barton."

"You," I called to another uniform. "Until the crime scene gets here, line up so no one can see the body. I don't need rumors starting. Where's the owner?"

"He's inside."

"Is he the one who found the body?"

"No. It was his kid bringing out the trash."

"I'll talk to them," I said as I patted the officer on the back.

My phone began ringing as I walked toward the front of the store.

"Barton," I answered.

"How bad is it?" The chief asked.

"Bad."

"Are we talking about a full-out gang war, bad?"

"Worse, Ted Bundy, bad."

I waited for the chief's response. After looking at my phone to see if he was still there, I continued, "I don't want to talk about any details out here. Let me wrap up with the scene, I'll be in after."

"Yeah," he sighed, then disconnected.

I entered the store to find a uniform posted near the door and the store owner, an older gentleman standing near a man who appeared to be sobbing. He was seated on a tall stool which I could only assume they sat on while tending the counter. Quickly, I surveyed the store, it was clean, neat and sparsely stocked. No surveillance cameras were visible.

Once I approached the men, the older man greeted me with a nod.

"I'm Detective Barton." I handed him one of my business cards as I spoke. "Can you walk me through what happened?"

"My name's Jeb. This here is my son David. We opened up like we always do. David was taking out the trash from the morning rush. He came running back in like he had seen a ghost." He spoke with words embodied by a southern drawl.

"What time do you open?"

"Seven a.m., and we close up about nine."

"Did you notice anything strange when you got here this morning? Any people hanging around?"

He furrowed his brow, tilting his head slightly, trying to recall.

"Naw," he responded as he shook his head.

"David..." I turned my attention to the son. "It's expected for you to be a little shaken after seeing something like that. Did you happen to recognize the woman?"

David shook his head with it still hanging. Observing his demeanor, I gathered he was probably trying his best to stave off a bit of shock.

"Jeb, we'll be out back taking pictures, gathering evidence, etc., for a while. If you think of anything, just come wave at me. But later on, just call if anything comes to you or David."

"Will do."

"If you could, keep what you saw to yourselves it would be great. I can recommend someone to talk to if you should need. As a matter of fact, here."

I dug my wallet from my pocket, flipped through the cards then handed them the card of the department trauma specialist.

"Much obliged," he said, nodding while taking the card.

"I'll be in touch with more questions. I know right now is not the best time."

He nodded in agreement then I made my way back to the gory scene. Just as I stepped outside the crime investigation van pulled up. George slid from the driver's seat of the van he'd parked at the side of the building.

"Where are we going?"

"Around back." I pointed as I walked by him.

He stopped at the back of the sprinter van, opening the door to retrieve his coveralls and tool kit. Jerry joined him in doing the same.

"What we got, Barton, gang banger?"

"Naw, another mother," I said solemnly.

Both George and Jerry stopped their motions in unison while looking at me with bulging eyes. All I could do was nod my head in acknowledgment of the unspoken question they were asking. Yes, I was serious. Yes, it's a mess. Yes, it's gruesome. Yes, even though this small town had never seen anything of this kind before, there was another one.

I dug in my pocket, retrieving another pair of gloves to replace the ones I'd discarded before going to talk to the owner. Without waiting for the crime scene investigating duo to gather their scruples, I headed to check the scene more closely. Just like with Marissa, this baby appeared to have been full term.

As I looked for the similarities and considered some of the same questions, I began to wonder where the hell Marissa's autopsy report was.

After checking the woman's pockets, I found nothing to identify her.

"Anybody find a purse?" I yelled.

"Right here," someone yelled back from inside the garbage dumpster.

He handed it out to an officer on the outside, who then handed it to me. I dug around in the bag, locating her ID. There was also a set of car keys. I looked around the lot, but I didn't see a car. Retrieving the fob from the bag, I pressed the panic button, but nothing happened. This reminded me that we still hadn't found Marissa's car either. There was no cell phone.

Pamela Justine was a twenty-five-year-old resident of Oklahoma City, according to her identification. What brought her to Lawton?

After searching around for a few other things, I jotted down some questions I had on my phone. I began my list of things we needed to know. But now, I needed to know if or how Marissa and Pamela were connected. Did it have something to do with their missing vehicles? How did they get to their prospective places of death? And even though their manners of meeting their ends were not the same, there were too many similarities for this not to have been the same killer.

Before heading into the office to update the chief, I gave George a few things to look out for. Plus, I went to check the front of the building. They needed to check the garbage bags out front. As I drove away, I noticed there was a discount store about a mile down. Taking a leap of faith, I pulled into their lot. Wouldn't you know, they had a camera. This might be a sliver of hope.

Chapter 3

"You are not about to tell me this."

I sat across from the chief in his office, looking at him in disbelief. He was the epitome of an insecure impostor afraid of doing any damn thing. I'd just explained to him the similarities between the two victims, and he refused to acknowledge that there was even a possibility they were connected.

"Chief, hear me out."

"I did. They weren't even killed the same way. Isn't that what usually qualifies a ser...you know."

He couldn't even say the phrase.

"Not all the time. There are people like—"

"It doesn't matter. We're not claiming that," he said, cutting me off.

"So then, what if it happens again?"

"It won't!"

"From your mouth to the air," I mumbled.

"What was that?"

"Nothing, I heard you," I said, then stood to leave.

Walking out of his office, leaving the door open, I didn't care if he wanted it closed. It was petty, but I didn't care. Our relationship had finally gotten to the point where we were cordial to one another, at best.

From my very first day, there'd been a haze of animosity surrounding Chief Saronson. He didn't like the fact that I didn't have to lick his bootstraps to get the job. And I didn't like the fact that he felt like I didn't deserve the position. I also got the impression it had more to do with the color of my skin than whether I had skills. But my criminal degree, test scores, and performance couldn't be denied.

I was at the top of my class at the academy. The degree I toted along with my college ROTC experience put me ahead of anyone else from the beginning. At times, I wanted to let the chief know that one day I'd be his boss. Instead, I let him be his true self so that I knew what I'd really be dealing with. That was one of the reasons I wanted to start my career this way. My aim was much higher than being a homicide detective, but I needed to see the inner workings for myself. Before achieving my true objective as District Attorney, I needed to know the strengths and weaknesses of the system. Chief Saronson was a definite weakness.

There were so many days I wanted to call him out on his bullshit. But, I bided my time. He wasn't blatantly racist like some of the folks in this little town, but I knew it was there. One of the reasons I thought long and hard about moving here after college was because of racism.

This was Oklahoma, once home to sundown towns, and we all know what happened in Tulsa. But hell, racism was everywhere. We can blame my wife for this choice, though.

She was a military brat. The last place they landed was Lawton. Her father was well-regarded and highly decorated, so much so that they let a Black man run the base. Though she hated the town, nothing made her prouder. But as teenagers go, she was full of rebellion. That's how she landed on the campus of Clark Atlanta University. She wanted to go as far away and as free as she could get. But for me, it was destiny.

When college was done, stage walks were performed, and it was time to go on to what life had to offer. I couldn't see my life without Serita. Oklahoma wasn't the plan. However, life had a different one. Shortly after graduation, Serita's father suffered a severe stroke. The eldest of three and pre-med, she felt it her duty to delay our plans to be his caregiver. She was never so selfish as to ask me to come with her or even wait for her. One of the things that made me fall in love with her was her conviction of standing on what was right rather than what was easy.

I could go into criminal justice anywhere. But I wouldn't be whole without Serita. She was my life from the day we met; there was no way I would allow her to leave me to navigate the world without her.

So, our plans changed to moving to Lawton, Oklahoma, instead of Detroit City, where I'd lived my whole life. I didn't have much family to speak of. My adoptive parents had both passed away two weeks into my senior year of high school. Their family, at best, tolerated me. I felt no kin to them. The way I saw it, there was nothing for me to go back to. Serita was my future. So, here we are.

"Boss, you alright?"

"No, Robin, I'm not."

"This may have your day looking up. We were finally able to obtain Marissa's bank records."

"You found something?"

"It looks like it. She received a $9000 deposit about seven months ago and has been receiving a $3000 deposit every month since."

"From?"

"A Robert Chatham."

"Where's his information?"

"Right here," she said, setting a sheet of paper on my desk.

"Why would a White man from Tuttle know a young Black college student, let alone pay her that much money?"

"I'm sure you're going to find out."

"I sure am," I said as I stood from the desk.

I plugged the address into my car's GPS once I was seated in it.

"Bixby, call The Boss."

"Hello," her melodic voice floated through my speakers as I pulled out of the parking space.

"Hey, baby. How's your day going?"

"Swimmingly, what's up?"

"I'm going to be home late."

"Ok. Is everything alright?"

"It's work."

"That didn't answer the question."

"I'm fine," I responded with a chuckle.

"Ok. Well, I'll cash in on my dinner raincheck with Tasha."

"Good, go have fun."

"You let me know when you're on your way home, ok?"

"Alright, say hello to your sister for me."

"Will do, I love you."

"Love you more."

I arrived in Tuttle an hour and a half later, after stopping for gas and some food. The city had a couple of attractions, a winery, a disc golf course, and a tiger safari. It was safe to say people came and went around there.

Pulling onto the street, it appeared to be a fairly recently formed subdivision. The lots were huge, however. The houses weren't anything to sneeze at either. Many of them were surrounded by privacy fences. After finding the address, pulling in the driveway, I climbed from my car. Casually, I headed to the door, and rang the bell. After waiting a few minutes, I hit the bell again and then returned to the car.

Just as I was about to climb behind the wheel, a woman called out from across the street.

"You lost?"

Hearing her words, I wasn't sure if I should take it as her trying to help me or if she was really asking what my n-word with an r ass was doing in her neighborhood.

"Just looking for Robert Chatham, ma'am," I called across the road, flashing her my badge.

"Oh, Suga, he's probably still down or at the high school."

"High school?"

"Yeah, he coaches the football team over there."

"Thank you," I said as I nodded, then got in the car.

You've got to love nosey neighbors.

Once I arrived at the high school football field, I parked but sat in the car for a moment. The two coaches had the players running drills. I found myself studying the men, trying to discern which one was indeed Mr. Chatham. In order to settle the bet with myself as to who was who, I finally climbed from the vehicle.

As I approached the field, many heads turned my way. I didn't want to stop their practice, but I wanted to be seen. So, I stood on the sideline with my hands resting atop the fence, watching the boys maneuver.

The coach looked my way, smiled then nodded. He got a head nod in return. Then his whistle sounded, he yelled then called a player over to him. They began walking toward me so I stood erect. Once they reached me the coach extended his hand.

"It is so nice to meet you. I'm glad you could come. Ronnie is doing an awesome job. I'll let you two catch up."

At first, I was confused, I'm sure the expression on my face displayed as much. But then number twenty-seven removed his helmet and I got it.

"He thinks I'm your dad?"

The young boy nodded with an obvious look of irritation.

"What's your name, son?"

"Ronnie Buchannon, sir."

"Is that Coach Chatham?"

"No, that's Coach Dukes. Chatham is the defense coordinator; he's over there," he stated with a point.

"Has Coach Dukes ever met your dad?"

"I think maybe once."

"Don't let them get to you. What position do you play?"

"Wide receiver, running back, sometimes safety."

"They can't catch you, huh?"

Ronnie shook his head with a smile.

"We may all look the same to some of them, but I tell you what, keep doing what you're doing, they'll remember your name." I placed my hand on his shoulder.

Ronnie nodded as if he'd had this conversation with someone before.

"My name is Gideon; Ronnie it was nice to meet you. I'm here to talk to Coach Chatham. But you keep up the good work. And don't be afraid to call your coach on his bullshit. But still be respectful." I winked with my last statement.

"Yes, sir," Ronnie said while placing his helmet back on.

I hung around the sideline until the practice was done. When Coach Chatham approached, I was a bit surprised. He wasn't a White man as I originally thought. He was a very fair-skinned Black man, perhaps of mixed race.

"Mr. Chatham?"

"Yes, may I help you?"

"I'm Detective Barton. I'd like to ask you a few questions," I said as I flashed my badge.

"Sure. How may I help you, officer?" he responded as he came to a stop in front of me.

"I need to ask you a few questions about Marissa Hannigan."

"What about her?"

The tone in his voice came off as a bit aggressive.

"When's the last time you spoke with her?"

"It was about a month ago, I guess."

"What's your relationship?"

"Relationship? We didn't have a relationship; we had a business arrangement."

"And what was the nature of your business?"

"What is this about?"

"We have uncovered several deposits you made to Marissa over the past few months. Can you tell me what they were for?

"Yeah, I did, and she ran off with it. Just tell her if she changed her mind, cool. I don't even care about the money, but my wife is devastated."

The mention of his wife threw me off a bit. Taking a different approach, less official, may help me get some things clear.

"Mr. Chatham, perhaps we should have a seat over there," I stated, pointing toward the bleachers.

He obliged; I followed. He sat then I sat next to him. Robert Chatham stared out at the field and began talking before I could.

"Something happened to her, didn't it?"

"Unfortunately."

"I had been trying to make myself believe she ran off with our money, more for my wife's sake. Somehow, deep down, I felt that wasn't true. She was the sweetest person."

"Can you clue me in as to what your dealings were with Marissa?"

"She was our surrogate."

That was something I had never considered. A light bulb went off in my head as a tear escaped his eye.

"So, the deposits were agreed-upon payments?"

"And medical expenses," he said as he nodded.

"Can you narrow down the day you last spoke?"

"Sure." He pulled out his phone, scrolling through his call log as he continued to explain, "She called after she left her last doctor's appointment. Here." He showed me the log.

I mentally noted the date and time.

"What did you guys talk about?"

"She said the visit went well. Wait, what about the babies?"

"I'm sorry..." I paused. "Did you say babies?"

"Yeah, she was having twins. How am I going to tell my wife?"

My visit to Mr. Chatham gave us much more than we were looking for. As soon as he let me in on his connection to Marissa, it opened new doors. And not very favorable ones. Not only were we to solve a murder, but now there's a missing baby. Immediately, I informed the chief of this. To his dismay, there was no choice but to call the FBI; kidnapping was their jurisdiction.

After breaking the news to Robert, I thought it would be best if we continued talking at his home. All this was not something he really wanted to tell his wife over the phone. And I had many more questions and much to discuss with them.

Once, he headed toward his house, I let him know I'd be shortly behind him. I thought it best if I got the local sheriff involved. It would prevent me from making this drive again if required, plus it didn't hurt to stave off any ill feelings between our two jurisdictions. So, I stopped at the Sheriff's office prior to going to have a talk with the Chathams. Surprisingly, the visit went much more smoothly than I expected.

When I arrived, Robert answered the door. His wife could be heard sobbing in the other room.

"Come on in. As you can imagine, my wife is upset. But she has questions, as do I. And we want to help as much as we can."

He took me in to see his wife. I was looking at a thirty-something blonde woman with blue eyes, not at all what I expected. She looked up, trying to dry her eyes. After giving my salutations and being offered a seat, I explained to them what we knew (the things I could share) and what we needed to know. Mr. Chatham gave me plenty of information. My hopes for this case perked up; it seemed we had viable leads. They knew where she had been, where she was going, etc. But they didn't know how or why she ended up in a hotel in Lawton.

"What about our baby?" Mrs. Chatham asked.

"It'll be the first priority. The FBI will be in touch with you. We would now have to classify part of this case as a kidnapping."

"I wasn't talking about that baby, the one th—"

She was unable to finish her sentence amid the wails she attempted to suppress.

"I'll have to speak with Marissa's parents regarding that."

"Is-was it a boy or a girl?"

"Girl."

"Excuse me." Mrs. Chatham left the room.

My focus went back to Mr. Chatham.

"Robert, I know this is hard. I just have a few more questions."

"Go ahead," he said as he nodded.

"Just to be clear. Marissa was a surrogate, your sperm, your wife's eggs?"

"I don't see what that has to do with any of this." He seemed offended.

"I'm just trying to determine if there's anyone else that may feel they have a right to the baby."

"Yes, my sperm, her eggs. We've experienced a few miscarriages. I didn't want Rebecca to go through that again."

I nodded as if I understood because I did.

"Where did you meet Marissa? Was it an agency?"

"No. One of Rebecca's colleagues. She's an administrator out at Langston."

My eyebrows raised at that statement.

"Professor Perry?"

"Yes, how did you know?"

"Just a lucky guess."

Writing in my notepad to make sure to follow up with the professor, I continued questioning him on things he knew. By the time I'd left the Chathams, there was a new hope growing within me.

These were actual leads, or at least prospective ones. Something way more than we'd had before. Like the fact that Marissa had an apartment off campus that apparently only the Chathams knew about. That was probably where her vehicle was parked. Robert Chatham had turned out to be a wealth of knowledge indeed.

Chapter 4

Just as expected, the chief was none too thrilled with the FBI blowing into town. They commandeered the small conference room in the station as their pseudo command center.

At first, I was apprehensive of the agents myself. Sadly, as an extreme minority in this town and department, it caused me to be on guard. There was always an underlying skepticism as to whether anyone I spoke with was a closeted racist. Shit or even a blatant one. But so far had been so good.

When Agent Jacoby arrived, there'd been a debrief set up. Robin and I, along with two other agents accompanying Jacoby sat in the conference room as the chief stood in front of us giving an overview. Before the chief could complete his summary of Marissa, Officer Smith burst into the office.

"Smith, can't you see we're busy?"

"I do. But—"

"But nothing, there better be a good reason why you're interrupting."

"There's another one, sir."

"Another, what?"

"Body," Smith responded with a look that said it was just as horrid.

Everyone scrambled to their feet.

"Are you ready to admit this *is* a serial now?" I asked the chief point-blank.

"What do you mean?" Agent Jacoby asked.

"This is the third one."

"I thought we were dealing with a murder and kidnapping. Why was the second victim not disclosed?"

"I-I was getting to that. But the victim was shot in a gang area. It was not the same," the chief responded confidently.

"Was there a baby involved?" Agent Jacoby inquired.

"Yes," Robin cut in before either one of us could respond.

"Chief Sarason, we should've been aware of this."

I made my way to my desk, grabbed my keys, and began out the door.

"I'm coming with you, detective," Jacoby shouted from the conference room entrance. As he walked toward me, he continued to give directions, "You two get all the information Ms. Gillette has. Then help her get a hold of whatever else she's waiting on."

As we sped to the scene, sirens blazing, I filled the agent in on the second victim along with the reason the chief didn't believe she was connected. We hadn't found her family yet, and weren't sure where she was originally from. And now, I had questions as to whether or not she also had a second missing child.

The scene we pulled up on was much like the other two. This woman's throat and wrists had been slit. She was found in a laundry mat bathroom. This victim had her throat slit from ear to ear while propped against the wall of the small restroom. She wore a dress that was soaked in blood. But in a similar fashion to the other victims, her fetus was now on display. Sadly, I was no longer ill at the sight of the gruesome display.

"He's trying to get someone's attention."

"Why do you say that?" Jacoby inquired.

My head snapped in his direction as if I were surprised. For a second, I was kind of talking to myself. It wasn't meant for him to hear. I don't normally have a partner. Momentarily, I'd forgotten he was there.

"Because he's getting bolder about where he's leaving them. Our first victim was behind closed doors, in a hotel. The likelihood of someone finding her quickly was slim. Outside of it, it was much easier for him to slip out without anyone else knowing there was any wrongdoing. But the second victim was left outside, behind a store, probably at night. The place is more likely to get her found much more quickly, but also hidden enough where maybe not. But this, a restroom in an establishment that is frequented daily, is more likely to be found right away."

"Excellent assessment, Barton," Jacoby commended.

I nodded acknowledging his acknowledgment, I couldn't help but to wonder what was really going through his mind. The statement was laced with a bit of surprise. I couldn't decide if it was because I was what he considered a small-town cop or if it was because I was a Black cop. He'd given me no reason to think he was one of those kinds. But again, this was Oklahoma.

What I soon figured out, Jacoby was assessing me to see how to approach our working relationship. Once he was confident I was competent, he began to voice his observations as well. As we went through the scene we worked pretty cohesively with one another.

Soon we were in a sort of see-saw rhythm of questions and where to go next. I admit it was a bit different working with a partner but it didn't feel forced. His insight and knowledge added to my own, in the end it was kind of refreshing to talk to someone other than myself.

We took care not to disturb anything as it was; we'd arrived before the medical examiner. Once we were satisfied, we saw everything we could with our naked eyes, and we headed to speak with the laundry attendant. Surely, she'd seen something; they had to have cameras.

"We'd like to review your surveillance footage."

"Sure thing. Come this way."

The attendant was a frail, older White woman with long, stringy blonde hair. She appeared to me the type that smoked two packs of

Marlboros per day and drank a pint every night. We followed her to a small office in the back that housed a small desk, old monitor and a small cot in the corner.

Just as she'd begun the recording from the top of the day, there was a commotion out front.

"Quick, get the paramedics here!" the medical examiner shouted.

"You go ahead, see what's going on. I'll keep reviewing the tape."

As I left the small space, people could be seen scurrying around. Sensing something urgent, I broke into a slight sprint toward the scene we'd just left.

"What's going on, Perkins?"

"This baby isn't gone."

I observed him wrap the small child in blankets while rubbing and blowing small breaths in its mouth. Momentarily. I was frozen, stunned. How could we miss that? How did none of the officers check that? Watching as the medical examiner attempted to restore the small being's vitality. For the first time in years, I found myself saying a silent prayer for the tiny soul that we thought had already been lost.

It seemed as if time had stopped as I stood transfixed on the medical examiner's actions. Suddenly, the tiny chest rose and fell at its own pace. A small cry woke me from my trance.

"What do I need to do?"

"We need to keep her warm until the paramedics get here."

Removing my jacket, I took the blood and mucus-covered miracle, placing it atop the medical examiner's jacket.

Jacoby appeared in the doorway with a look of shock, which we were all feeling at this point. Looking up at him, our eyes met. We both had similar expressions. I wondered if he was thinking what I was.

"Did you see anything on the tape?" I asked.

"Yes, but not really. The perp wore a hoodie pulled over his head, gloves, and a surgical mask. The attendant remembered seeing them, but didn't think anything of the mask. You know, COVID and all."

"He can't have been gone too long or too far."

Jacoby looked at his watch. Then noted the time. "It's nine-thirty, the place opened at seven."

"We got the call almost an hour ago," I pointed out.

"He could still be watching."

"What's taking the paramedics so long?" I wondered.

I'd grown increasingly anxious. There was a precious life in my hands, a killer possibly right outside. We had no answers, and still had at least one missing baby.

"I'll drive," Jacoby stated.

Without a second thought, we headed for the exit.

"Let Memorial know we're on the way," I called out to one of the uniforms as we passed by.

I climbed into the back of my car with the precious cargo as Jacoby jumped into the driver's seat. As we pulled out of the parking lot and headed for the hospital, I scanned all the random faces I could see.

"I didn't see any hoodies or masks in the crowd," Jacoby acknowledged.

"No. I wouldn't suspect we would, but I scanned the faces. If I see one of them again, I'll know."

He turned on my lights and siren as I gave him directions to the hospital.

Chapter 5

As we sat in what was now the situation room, I couldn't stop thinking about my morning.

When my alarm blared, I'd already been lying there staring at my wife for at least an hour. I was failing at leaving work at work.

"How long are you going to stare at me?" she questioned without opening her eyes.

I'd reached back, hitting the snooze without taking my eyes off her. Her glow was what I needed.

"Can you see through your eyelids?"

"No, but I can feel you staring at me," she said as her eyes popped open.

"I can't help it. You're just so beautiful."

"You're not fooling me. What's wrong?"

"Nothing, I can't admire my gorgeous wife?"

"You can, you do. But I know when you have something on your mind."

"How much I love you is on my mind."

"I'm not buying it. Which tells me it has something to do with work. I know how you feel about bringing work home. But you know I'm here for you for whatever reason. If you need to talk, I'm willing to listen."

"Nothing to worry your pretty little head about," I said before placing a kiss on her forehead.

"Offer still stands," she said before rolling over to get out of bed.

I watched as she waddled into the bathroom.

"What time is your appointment, again?"

"Two. If you can't make it, I understand."

"I'll be there."

"Barton," Jacoby snapped me out of my head.

I hadn't heard anything they'd said in the last five minutes.

"Sorry. I was thinking, it's likely he was watching yesterday and possibly all the other scenes."

"Likely," Jacoby agreed.

"We have requested access to Marissa's medical records," Robin chimed in.

"I still want to go to the clinic to ask what questions I can. They may have insight as to how Marissa left. And maybe a face-to-face will help with some answers. I know there are some answers they can't legally give us. But body language and facial expressions say a lot."

"I agree," Jacoby nodded.

"Also, we may be able to find out if victim number three was also a patient."

"We were able to identify the latest vic. Won't hurt to see if she was a patient as well," Jacoby added.

"We should have all requested phone records soon. We'll spend time going through that," Mason, one of Jacoby's colleagues, stated.

"I'm working on tracking down Marissa's vehicle. The order came through late yesterday. I'll be following up with OnStar," Robin interjected.

"Let's get to it," Jacoby said as he stood.

After the day we had yesterday, I guess it was a given he was coming with me. Whether I wanted it or not, I had a partner.

"I can drive today if you want?"

"Being a passenger is a little foreign to me. Besides, I just have to tell you where to go. I'll drive," I explained.

He chuckled as we walked out of the building, then climbed into my ride.

"Hopefully, we get some answers or a new road to travel with this clinic," Jacoby declared.

"That's what I'm wishing for."

"You know, what you said about him watching, I was thinking the same. I want to go over all video footage again."

"And any crime scene photos that were taken just in case he can be spotted in the crowd."

"I like the way you think, Barton. You ever considered the bureau?"

"Honestly, no. I have my eye on a bigger, maybe not bigger, but different prize."

"Do tell."

I hesitated. I'd never shared my career goals with anyone but my wife.

"DA," I spat out.

"Really? I guess I can see that. But I don't know. You have a head for the investigation. Are you sure you can give up the action?"

I laughed.

"This is the most action I've seen since I've been here."

"You're a natural, though. We could use someone like you."

"Hadn't really given it any thought. It's something to think about."
The car rolled to a stop. "We're here."

"That was quick."

"How big do you think Lawton is?" I questioned with a chuckle.

"May I help you?" the receptionist greeted us when we approached the
counter.

"We'd like to speak with the office manager, please," I said, showing
her my badge.

"Sure. One second."

She got up from her seat, retreating to somewhere else beyond the
reception area door.

We both stepped aside while looking around the small lobby. My ears
were queued to listen for any words spoken in hushed tones. While I
could see Jacoby slyly trying to peer at the sign in sheet.

The door opened to the inner part of the clinic.

"Gentlemen, I'm Mrs. Harper. Come right this way."

We followed her down the hall as we passed a few open exam rooms.
She led us to an office in the back corner.

"Please have a seat. How may I help you, officers?"

"I'm Detective Barton. This is Agent Jacoby. We're here to ask a few questions about a patient, Marissa Hannigan."

"As I'm sure you're aware. I can't give you much information in accordance with HIPAA laws."

"We're working on that. But our questions aren't specific to her medical history as of now," Jacoby chimed in.

"Our questions are more for her state of mind and demeanor at her last appointment."

"What was her name again?" she questioned as she positioned her hands over her computer keyboard.

"Marissa Hannigan."

Mrs. Harper click-clacked her fingers on the keyboard.

"It looks like there are two people on duty today who were here at her last appointment. I can have them come speak with you."

"Perfect," Jacoby declared.

She nodded, then walked out of the office to go retrieve whomever she was referring to.

A middle-aged White woman stepped into the office with a not-so-pleasant look on her face.

"Hello, you are?" I questioned.

"Debra Holt."

"Ms. Holt, we were wondering if you could answer a few questions for us."

"I don't know; it depends on what you're asking."

"You remember this woman?" Jacoby questioned, showing her a picture of Marissa.

"Yeah."

"Can you tell us how she seemed at her last appointment?"

"She seemed fine to me." She shrugged.

I couldn't help but notice that the irritation apparent in her voice when she spoke with me seemed nonexistent when speaking to Jacoby.

"Without any specifics, was there anything that may have upset her at the last appointment? Anything out of the ordinary?" Jacoby asked.

"Not that I can think of."

"Would you happen to know if she drove herself to and from the appointment?" I questioned.

It took her a minute to answer. I would've liked to think she was thinking about it. But my gut was telling me she just didn't want to answer my questions. She didn't even look my way when she finally spoke.

"Not that I know of. We didn't talk much."

"Thanks for your time," Jacoby uttered.

When she left, we shared a look but said nothing. He knew what it was. But I started to wonder if there was more she would've said if I weren't there. What could she have said? Who knows?

When the receptionist walked in, the energy about her was lighter.

"Hi..." I paused as she filled in the blanks for us.

"Bianca."

"Bianca, I'm Detective Barton, this is Agent Jacoby we have a few questions about a patient."

Jacoby held out his phone, showing her the same picture of Marissa.

"Do you remember this woman?"

"Marissa, of course. She was such a sweetheart. Did something happen to her?"

It was then that I realized how good a job we'd done of keeping these things under wraps. And then a bit of shock surfaced in this small ass town where everyone talked. They weren't talking about this. Did they really not know or just not care because all the victims so far were Black?

"Unfortunately, Ms. Hannigan was killed a few weeks ago."

"Oh my! Her babies?"

Neither of us said anything. And she began to cry.

"Can you tell us anything about her last visit? Did she seem herself?" I questioned.

"No," she shook her head. "She seemed fine. I mean she mentioned being tired, but we laughed about it because it was almost time to evict those babies and she was as big as a house."

"Did she drive herself?" Jacoby inquired.

"She did. But now that you mention it. I think she took one of those cards from the front counter. There are a couple of transportation services that come and leave cards here."

"That might be very helpful. Can you show us?"

"Sure."

We followed her out of the office, down the hall, and into the lobby.

"Here they are."

"Wait." Jacoby stopped her before she touched any of the cards. "Can you just point to the one she took?"

"I'm not sure which one she picked up. I just remember her hovering here a little bit."

"Thank you very much, Bianca." I fished a rubber glove from my pocket, then gathered all the cards that were present.

"We'll be in touch if there are any more questions," Jacoby said to Ms. Harper, who just happened to be standing on the other side of the counter.

Once we made it back to my vehicle, I retrieved an evidence bag from my trunk and deposited the cards into it.

"What's next?" Jacoby questioned once we were seated in the car.

I looked up from my phone after checking my messages.

"Get these to the lab for prints, then help with those phone records that have finally come through."

"And pray there isn't another body before we do."

Just as I was about to pull out of the parking space, my phone rang.

"What's up, Robin?"

"We found Marissa's van. Head to Thomas Brothers towing."

I hit the lights and siren. We made it to the yard in record time.

Chapter 6

IT WAS LATE WHEN I finally got home. I tried to quietly slip into bed after I'd showered. But my attempt to not wake Serita was in vain.

"You forgot."

"I did, but I didn't."

"What the hell does that even mean?"

She slowly rolled over to face me.

"It had slipped my mind for a second. Then, when I remembered and looked at the time, I couldn't step away from work. I'm sorry."

"It's alright. I told you, you didn't have to come."

"But I wanted to. It's not ok. We're in this together, and I want to show up for you."

"You are here for me. For us."

Serita cupped her hand on my cheek while staring into my eyes to let me know she was ok. It was what she did to reassure me, to calm my racing thoughts without saying anything. She grounded me. It was her way of saying she loved me without saying it. Closing my eyes, I nodded, took a deep breath and calmed. She turned back to her side while grabbing my hand to wrap around her waist.

She snuggled closer to me as I let my hand rest on her belly. That's how I have always fallen asleep. Usually quickly. But tonight was a different story. I lay there still trying to rid my thoughts of today's activities long after she'd fallen into her rhythmic cadence.

My head was swirling with the things that had transpired throughout the day. What we discovered at the tow yard gave us some insight along with more questions. It seems, Marissa's van had two flat tires. It was found on the side of the road and had been impounded by the Oklahoma Highway Patrol.

Upon further inspection, it appeared her tires had been tampered with. There was a nail in each of them. And in any other circumstance, it may not have been suspicious. But two tires at once. Our working theory was that she'd been targeted. But why exactly? When and for how long had she been followed?

According to the records of the tow yard, her vehicle was towed two days after we found her body. How long had it been there before it was found? We had to wait for forensics to go through all the samples they'd taken from the vehicle. Maybe we'd get lucky. Perhaps her assailant left a print on the car, in the car? Was he ever in her car? Did she call someone?

But more pressing than that, I couldn't get the baby out of my head. I'd held that precious life. A life we almost didn't catch. Before coming back home, I had to stop by the hospital to check on her. They say she was a fighter, and that was evident. She wasn't out of the woods yet, but the doctors were optimistic. Knowing that helped to settle my guilt. How could we have missed that?

My effort to clear my head proved to be futile. The more I tried not to think of the case, the more things I considered. Soon, there was a list forming in my head. The things we knew, the things we still needed to know, the things we needed to question, the things we were still waiting on, were all on the list. I landed on what would be my priority in the morning. Well, in the very early hours, the numbers on my watch glowed 0300 hours.

I sat in the make-shift situation room Robin had constructed in one of the back offices. I'd just taken a sip of my coffee.

Jacoby appeared in the doorway.

"Did you sleep?"

"Barely."

"Why are you here so early?"

"Can't sleep anyway." I shrugged.

"Same. I just left the hospital."

I nodded. "I went last night."

He nodded in response. "So, what are we doing here?"

"I'm going to go through this surveillance footage that we finally received from the discount store not too far from where the second victim was found."

"What are you looking for?" Jacoby questioned.

"Not sure. Hopefully, something jumps out at me."

"Maybe the perp drove by there and stopped in," he added.

"Something," I stated with an exasperated breath.

"While you do that, I'll go over some of these crime scene photos with fresh eyes."

"Robin is putting together a request for the warrant to get the clinic to release records to us," I disclosed.

"And I had a rush put on anything collected from the van," he informed.

"I've been thinking about the van, her tires."

"Someone had to have picked her up, right?"

"Yeah." He waited for me to continue my thought. "She would've called someone she knew, right?"

"Possibly, but who?"

"The only man we know who knew her is Mr. Chatham."

"But his phone records don't show she called him."

"Neither did hers. There weren't any calls made after she spoke with the Chathams," I stated.

"What if their phone call didn't go the way they said?"

"It's a possibility. But I didn't get that from them."

"If she didn't call anyone, how did she get from the side of the road to that hotel?" he questioned.

"Let's say, they orchestrated the tires, followed her, waited, then pulled up like a good Samaritan."

"She would've been grateful."

"But would she have gotten in the car with them? A stranger?" I wondered aloud.

"Someone she knew?"

"Possibly," he responded.

"We need that warrant. We need to find something in that van. I hate to say, it's a waiting game," he admitted.

"I just hope we're not waiting for another body."

Chapter 7

We had gone over every aspect of the evidence and nothing significant stuck out. An amber alert had been issued for the baby. I let Jacoby be the face on the news stations. None of them wanted to say it but by my assumption, his White face would more than likely garner more attention than mine. And even though he didn't say it. He was thinking the same thing as me. That was evident when he didn't give a description of the baby. His report was ambiguous.

He'd just informed everyone to be on the lookout for a newborn. Possibly abandoned. Jacoby reported that there was evidence of foul play and cautioned people to question anyone they knew who just showed up with a baby. There was no mention of the mothers being murdered. No mention of multiple victims. Just be on the lookout for a newborn. The masses weren't aware that it may be more than one baby. Shit, we weren't sure there'd be more than one.

I hoped there was only one.

As I sat at my desk trying to figure out what the next angle to investigate was, my desk phone rang. As soon as it did, my stomach dropped. I was afraid to answer it. My phone hadn't rung this much since I'd been on duty here. And in the last few weeks, every time it did, the news wasn't so great.

"Barton," I answered.

There was no response.

"Hello?"

Nothing. I sat trying to hear anything in the background. I picked up on some faint breathing, but that was it. Waving my hand, I tried to get Robin's attention. Just when she looked my way, they hung up.

"What's up?" she asked after stepping to my desk.

"I think that was him."

"What makes you think that?"

I shrugged. "A feeling. But it could've very well been a prank call."

"What did they say?"

"Nothing. That's just it. They didn't hang up right away like they'd realized they'd dial the wrong number. Just breathing, then click."

Robin's brows furrowed. "I'll see if we can get a trace."

She turned on her heels and was gone before I could utter my next thought.

If it were him, that means he's watching.

Jacoby and one of his counterparts took a ride to speak with the Chathams. I'd gone back through the crime scene photos. We were all spinning our wheels, knowing there had to be something we were missing. Something that was right in front of us. A question we weren't asking.

The medical records might help, but I wasn't hanging on that to bust the case wide open. What dots we needed to connect the victims. The fact that all three had been near-term pregnancies seemed less than random. It was baffling; we'd confirmed neither of the other victims was a patient at the same clinic. That would be the obvious path, but it wasn't there.

Our second victim, Pamela, was a resident of Guthrie. How she ended up behind a convenience store nearly two hours away is unknown. We'd yet to get in contact with anyone to notify them of her passing. She was not a student at Langston either. So, there's no connection there. And we've yet to identify the third victim; her ID was not left for us like the others. There's some significance to that, but I don't know what yet.

So far, we've done a great job of keeping things under wraps. But I knew it was only a matter of time before something got leaked. And honestly, though it would be chaos, maybe the public involvement would help move things along. Maybe it would help us identify victim number three. Perhaps, by a long shot, a witness would come forward. And maybe going public would prevent there being a fourth victim.

All these things are possibilities but what's for sure, it would cause widespread panic.

"Boss."

Robin had a look on her face, I couldn't quite read.

"The trace came back?"

"No. Not yet. There's...there's..." She hesitated. "Randy came to me with some concerns."

"About?"

"There's a woman out in the lobby who's looking for her daughter."

"Ok. What's the problem?"

"Randy says that Sargent Black is stalling; he just thinks the girl ran away."

"Why should I be concerned about a runaway?"

"Randy thinks it may be Jane."

Jane. That's what we'd been calling victim number three.

"Where is she now?"

"I had him show her to room five."

"Thank you, Robin."

When I entered the small interview room, the woman on the other side of the table looked up at me with tired eyes. It looked as if she hadn't slept in days. There was worry and sadness on her face. She took a sip of the water Robin had given her. I suspect out of nervousness more than thirst.

"Good morning, I'm Detective Barton. You're here to report your daughter missing, is that right?"

"Yes. I haven't heard from her in days. I tried calling."

"I take it this isn't something she does often."

"Not lately, Crystal has had trouble in her past, but she got herself together."

"When you say trouble."

"Drugs."

I nodded in understanding.

"But she's been clean for 'bout three years. She wouldn't touch anything now."

"What makes you so sure? Addicts fall off the wagon all the time."

"'Cause, she ain't just clean for herself this time. She pregnant."

"When's the last time you spoke with her?"

"It's been four days. She called me about six in the morning."

"Does she call you every morning?"

"We talk every day. Especially since she coming up on her due date. I'm scared she went into labor and something happened. I done called the hospitals but they won't tell me nothing. They's talking about some Hippo or some shit. I just want to know my daughter and them babies are ok."

"Babies?"

"Yeah, she having twins. My momma was a twin but like they say stuff like that be skipping generations, you know? I didn't have twins. Just Crystal, she all I got. And them babies. She loved them babies. I know she ain't do nothing that'll hurt them babies. It's something wrong. I just came to see if the hospitals a tell y'all something 'cause they won't tell me."

"Does your daughter live in Lawton?"

"Yes. She stay right over there off Bishop and seventeenth."

"Do you have a picture of your daughter, Ms?"

"Elkins. Beverly Elkins."

She picked up her cell phone, pressed the screen a few times, then turned her phone to me.

"I'll be right back."

Before she could register what I said, I was out the door. I stalked over to Robin's desk.

"I need you to call Jacoby, get him back here. Call the grief counselor."

I paused to think about who and what else we needed.

"It's her?" Robin's tone was solemn.

With a nod, I responded. My facial expression matched her tone. But I didn't have time to reflect on that; there was something more pressing. We had another baby to find, which meant so many more things and so many more unanswered questions. I needed as much out of Ms. Elkins as I could gather before all hell broke loose.

"Send the counselor in when they get here. I'm going to try to get as much information out of her as I can before we give notification."

"Yes, Boss."

Robin picked up her phone to make the necessary calls while I went to my desk. I grabbed the manilla folder, a legal pad for notes then took a deep breath before I went back into the interview room.

"Ms. Elkins." I sat in front of her, pen and paper in hand. She knew I was taking this seriously. "Tell me about the last time you spoke with your daughter."

I listened intently as she recounted that morning. Writing down times and places her mother knew she'd been going.

"You say she had a doctor's appointment. Do you know the doctor's name or the clinic?"

"Yeah, she went to Dr. Chambers over there on Lee Blvd. But that ain't where she was going. She was going to see some other kinda doctor. Some kinda specialist 'cause her suga was high."

"You know where that was?"

"Naw, I ain't think to ask."

"I'm going to need your daughter's telephone number, address, and write down the kind of car she drives."

I slid a piece of paper I'd torn from my pad to her with a pen.

"Thank you so much for helping me."

That statement made my stomach do a flip. She wouldn't be thanking me in a few minutes.

"Can you think of anywhere else she might go?"

Just as she was about to answer, there was a knock at the door.

"One moment," I said to the knocker. "I'll be right back. Write those things down for me."

When I stepped into the hallway, I shut the door behind me. Before I could go any further, I took a deep breath. I knew everything in that room was about to change.

"Ms. Elkins, this is Officer Cameron."

She nodded then looked at me with a questioning gaze. She wanted to know why there was someone else stepping into the room.

"Hello, Ms. Elkins."

Officer Cameron extended his hand and then sat down. I took the seat next to him.

"She's dead, ain't she?"

Beverly Elkins waited for me to answer with tear-brimmed eyes.

"Ms. Elkins, I'm sorry to say, based on the picture you've shown me, I have reason to be certain your daughter is deceased."

She nodded as she let the tears fall from her eyes.

"Whe...when did this happen? And where was she?"

"She was found four days ago in a laundromat restroom. It was early morning. From what you've told me, whatever happened must've happened right after you spoke with her."

"Can you think of anyone who may have wanted to hurt her? What about the baby's father? Is he in the picture? Any problems with him?"

"I can't say. She wouldn't talk about him. Just said she was raising her babies without him."

"Was there anybody from her old life?"

Beverly shook her head.

"She never said anything about anybody after her or anything."

"And you're sure she was alone when you talked to her?"

"Yeah, as far as I know. She said she was up early. She was going to the doctor. We talked about what she ate for breakfast. And then she told me she was going to call me later. I ain't heard from my baby after that. I can't believe her and the babies are gone."

She let out an audible sob.

"Ms. Elkins, about the babies. One of them survived; she's at Memorial. Officer Cameron here will escort you over to the hospital shortly. And..." I paused to brace myself.

Somehow, it felt harder to tell her one of her grandchildren was missing than it did to let her know her daughter was gone. Perhaps it was because I feared we'd never find her. I cleared my throat.

"There's something else. The other baby wasn't at the scene."

"What you mean? They took her? Why would they only take one?"

"Ms. Elkins, I assure you, I aim to find out."

"Y'all knew this when I walked in here. You stringing me along. Find my granddaughter."

As she yelled at me, she stood snatching the bag she had with her close to her chest. I stood with her.

"I wasn't stringing you along. I just wanted to get all the information from you that I could. I promise you, I want to find your daughter, and until today, we weren't aware of a second baby. We didn't know her name until you showed me that picture. I'm sorry for your loss. I'm going to do everything I can to find your granddaughter. I'm sorry."

She stopped just before the door.

"I don't need an escort. You just call them people and tell them I'm coming to get my baby. I pray you mean what you say, Detective. In this town, I expect them not to care. I hope you're better than them."

Chapter 8

I SENT OFFICER CAMERON to follow Ms. Elkins in his vehicle regardless of what she said. The hospital staff would need verification of her claims in order to allow her to see the baby anyway.

I couldn't focus on the last part of her statement either. Did I know what she was getting at, yes. But my mind couldn't afford to lend any part of it to anger about this racist place. Crystal was my focus. Now that we have her name we can try a few more searches.

"What's up?" Jacoby said as he walked up to my desk.

"Victim number three is Crystal Elkins. She's from right here in Lawton. She's local. I'd bet anything that's why she didn't have ID."

"He needed time to get that baby somewhere." I pointed at him.

"Exactly!"

"So, maybe she wasn't planned, some exigent circumstance."

"That would explain the difference; she wasn't on display, her ID, the scene not being as neatly staged."

"What else do we know?"

"Crystal was also having twins. He's taking one baby. More than likely, Pamela was having twins, too. We've probably got three missing babies."

"I can't keep a lid on this whole thing anymore. And you need to be there. They can't just see me; you are a major part of this investigation."

We'd spent the rest of the day reorganizing and rearranging our evidence, clues, and timeline. Just trying to find another opening, an avenue to answers. We hadn't come up with much to get us closer to solving any of this. If anything, there were more questions.

Then, after the press conference, there were a number of things to put in place.

A tip line was set up. Additional patrols were added around the city. We needed more bodies now that the case had more eyes on it. It had become national news. They, the reporters, had given him a name: The Gemini Killer.

I tried to slip in so as not to disturb Serita's sleep, but she had other plans.

"I saw you on TV today."

I jumped at her voice. "Shit, Serita. You startled me. I didn't expect you to be up."

When I walked over to her, placing a kiss on her forehead, she gave me the side-eye.

"Why didn't you tell me about this case?"

"Since when do I ever tell you about my cases?"

"I know you got this whole keep work at work thing, but a killer on the loose is something you should've told me about."

Her logic was sound. I did what I always do when she's right and I'm wrong. Said nothing.

"Gideon, are you seriously gonna stand there and not say a word?"

"You're right. I apologize. To be honest, my focus was more on not worrying you than warning you."

"So, tell me the truth. How long have you been sitting on this?"

I shrugged. "A wee—"

"A week?" She cut me off.

"Or two or three."

"Gideon!"

Placing my hands on her hips, I pulled her body to mine. While positioning her so that I could wrap my arms around her from the back, I whispered in her ear.

"You know I would never let anything happen to you, either one of you," I said as I rubbed her swollen belly.

"According to that press conference, all pregnant women should be cautious. I don't think a killer would make exceptions for the lead detective's wife."

"You know we can't give all the details in a press conference. In truth, you don't meet the criteria. You're not near-term being the most prevalent."

"What else?"

"Serita, I really don't want to burden you with that. My baby doesn't need to hear all the gory details even though his mother may want to."

"He, huh? You don't know it's a boy. It could be a beautiful girl."

"As long as either one of them is happy, healthy, and ours, it doesn't matter."

"You remember my ultrasound appointment in the morning, right?"

"Uhhhh...yeah."

She snickered as she pulled from my embrace, and she faced me.

"It's early at eight."

"Good. I can take you. I'll just go in later, tomorrow."

"I'm going to bed," she said before kissing me on the lips.

"I'm going to unwind a bit, then I'll be up. Goodnight, babe."

"If you didn't eat, there's a plate for you in the fridge.

"Love you."

"You better," she responded before padding up the stairs.

"Gideon. Gideon."

Feeling her taps on my leg woke me up. It took me a few seconds to come to my senses.

"Why are you on the couch?"

"By the time I was ready to lay it down, I didn't want to chance waking you up."

"Honey, that's considerate, but you can't possibly get a good night's sleep lying across the couch. Just come to bed next time."

"What time is it?"

"Time to get up and dressed. I can't be late for this appointment."

After I was able to focus my eyes, I took in my wife's beauty. She had always been and was still the prettiest thing in the world to me. It didn't matter what she was dressed in. Even in a bathrobe, the way she glowed made me want her, instantly.

"We can save time with a shower together."

She looked at me blankly. I gave her a sly smile in return.

"I said, I can't be late. There's nothing quick about showering with you, sir. That's how I got this way," she said, pointing at her belly.

I chuckled, shrugged, then stood. "I tried."

"You did. Besides, I already showered. Get to moving."

After showering and getting myself together, I grabbed the travel coffee mug sitting on the counter.

"Thanks for the coffee."

"That wasn't for you. It was for me."

"Ma'am...no coffee for that boy in your belly."

"I can't wait until they tell us it's a girl today," she said with an exaggerated roll of her eyes.

"Whatever."

"The coffee wasn't for me to drink. It was so you wouldn't fall asleep driving me this morning."

"Jokes, you're full of jokes."

It took me a little time to get ready and we were soon on our way. It wasn't until we were in the car that I let the excitement seep in. I was getting a glimpse of my offspring. My legacy.

"No, don't turn here."

"But this is the way to your Dr.'s office."

"It would be if that's where we were going. The ultrasound is at Transparent Images."

"Huh?"

"Some of these smaller clinics partner with an imaging center. It saves them money by preventing them from having to buy the equipment or employ technicians. They do all the imaging. Like X-rays, MRIs, CTs, and ultrasounds."

I nodded, she went on talking. But I didn't hear her. It dawned on me. What if our victims all went to the same imaging center.

"Is this the only imaging center in Lawton?"

"Yeah, there's one in Wichita Falls and, of course, in Oklahoma City."

She continued to give me the directions, but my head filled with a thousand more questions. Not for her but for the cases. I dropped her at the entrance then parked the car. But before making my way into the building, I made a phone call.

"Hey, Boss," Robin answered.

"Hey, we need to check to see if any of the victims were sent to..." I looked at the name of the building. "Transparent Images."

"Got it. Anything else?"

"Not now. I'll be there in a couple of hours."

"See you then."

Serita was seated in the waiting room when I walked in. Just when I was about to take a seat next to her, they called her name. After helping her to her feet, I followed her back to the exam room. As the nurse instructed her, I felt nervous. Ironic, I wasn't the one with a baby growing inside me but I was nervous.

It wasn't long after she'd undressed and got on the exam bed that another nurse or tech knocked on the door.

"Hey there."

"Hello," we responded in unison.

She strolled over to the machine that sat at the side of the bed.

"This won't be cold, we'll warm it up. Let's see what we have here."

The blonde, blue-eyed woman said all this while squeezing a clear jelly on my wife's belly. She seemed cheerful and friendly. I watched the screen of that machine intently as if I could tell what I was looking at. But I really couldn't.

"There's the head."

We watched as our tiny human came into view. Head, a hand, I could see a foot.

"And…" She moved the wand thing around, then tapped the buttons on her screen. "There looks like…" She paused again.

"Is something wrong?" I had to ask.

"That depends."

"On?"

An 'A' appeared on the screen, she tapped the keys some more then a 'B' appeared.

"On if you're prepared for twins."

"WHAT!"

"Yeah, looks like there are two of them in there."

"That explains why I am larger than life already."

"Let's see if we can get the sex of both these little buggers."

"Oh my! We have to rearrange the nursery."

"Have you painted it yet?"

"No."

"Well, you can surely go with a shade of blue."

"You mean…"

"They're both boys. Let me get you some pictures."

Serita and the tech were having a conversation all on their own. I'd checked out. We were having boys. Twins...Twins. Shit. Twins.

After that it seemed like everything sped up, it wasn't because it actually had but more because I was somewhere else. My mind went down a hundred roads while they finished up. Serita dressed and I followed her out into the lobby to check out.

As she stood there talking to the receptionist, I noticed the business cards on the counter. One stuck out. It was the same transportation service as the clinic where Marissa was a patient. Very interesting.

"Just fucking check again!"

Robin stood next to my desk, looking at me like I'd lost my mind. And maybe I had.

"I'm sorry, Robin. I didn't mean to snap at you."

"You better be." She turned on her heels. I felt bad.

"Is everything alright with you?" Jacoby asked.

I shook my head. The time had come when I could no longer keep my private and professional life separated. Merging the two was not something I wanted to do. I'd kept my personal life away from the job for a number of reasons. But not trusting these racist fuckers was number one. If there was anyone to trust here, it's Robin. And Jacoby had turned out to be someone that I'd bet on.

"There's something we need to discuss. Can you grab Robin and meet me in the situation room?"

When they came in, I was standing next to the whiteboard. The situation room was nothing more than a small office we'd commandeered. All the clues, hypothesis, evidence, crime scene photos, the entire case was on that whiteboard.

"We're here," Jacoby said as he crossed the threshold.

"Close the door, please."

He looked at me curiously. There wasn't like there were many people in the office and the walls were windows. But I didn't want anyone but them to hear what I had to say.

"Earlier, I found this card at the clinic I took my wife to."

I pointed out the transportation card.

"We figured he probably leaves those at all doctors' offices," Jacoby interjected.

"Yeah, but this was at an imaging clinic. They only handle X-rays, MRIs, CTs, stuff like that, and ultrasounds."

"You think he got his victims from there?" Robin said.

"It would be the only thing to connect them all."

"We've tried to track the number; it seems to be a call app. There hasn't been a response to any of the messages I left," Robin said.

There was a knock on the door, and I waved Officer Cameron in.

"I've asked Officer Cameron here. What I'm about to say is that I'd like to keep it between the four of us as much as we possibly can..." I paused waiting for confirmation from them. They all nodded then I continued. "My wife and I are expecting."

"Congrats!" Jacoby said.

"Awe...how sweet," Robin said.

"That's the best," Cameron stated.

"I found out today that we're having twins."

All their smiles faded.

"Officer Cameron, if you're up for it, I'd like you to shadow her daily."

"You got it, Boss."

"It goes without saying that the need to find this guy has just amplified," Jacoby said.

"The state license administration has that business registered to a Travis Moore," Robin said. "But I haven't been able to find anything else in that name. No DMV record, no utility record, nothing—"

"Not in Lawton, anyway," Jacoby interjected.

"Right, and there's more than a thousand Travis Moores in the phone number registry."

"Cameron. You can dress in plain clothes. Here's my address. She knows you're coming."

He took the piece of paper I was handing to him. Telling him she hated the idea was irrelevant, so I didn't.

"I'm on it," he said as he made his way out of the office.

"There has to be a way to narrow down the pool of Travis Moores."

Bam

The door slammed against the wall as it was pushed open. We all looked at Saronson.

"There's another body."

Chapter 9

We arrived at a boarded-up building. It was what used to be a daycare that had been closed for what looked like some time. The reporters' vans had beaten us there. The police tape surrounded the whole of the property. Once we were let in, we pulled up to the back of the location. The vegetation around the building, parking lot and playscape was overgrown.

Jacoby and I stepped out of the vehicle. An officer walked over to brief us.

"The victim is over at the monkey bars. It was called in by a homeless man."

"Where is he?" I asked.

"We have him over there." He pointed to the other side of the street. "I had Johnson go get him a sandwich. He'll hang around to talk to y'all."

"Good. Thanks."

We headed over to the area where the body had been found. There was something about the way the overgrown trees loomed over the space. It made it seem dark, eerie and isolated. I felt closed in, not at all as if we were outside. My eyes scanned the landscape as we roamed through. The further we ventured, the more uneasy I felt.

As the small playscape area came into view, I stopped in my tracks. I almost lost my lunch. Again! And I hadn't even had lunch yet. There she was suspended in the air, tied to the monkey bars as if it were her crucifix. She was still clothed in a short dress. And the baby...the baby was still attached by its umbilical cord hanging from her center.

It wasn't until Jacoby doubled back to ask if I was alright that I realized I'd closed my eyes. Nodding to answer his question, I willed the tears forming to retreat.

"It'll be understandable if you want to sit this one out."

After shaking my head, I forced my eyes open.

"No. I'm good. Let's get this over with."

Jacoby looked at me with sympathy, and I wasn't sure how I felt about it. Looking him square in the eyes, I nodded, then continued the path to our corpse. There was a bag at her feet, which appeared to be a tote, probably her purse. There was no blood pooled beneath where she hung. Meaning, she wasn't killed there. She'd been brought to this location. Why?

After taking in the scene in front of me, I moved to inspect the contents of the tote, careful not to move it out of place. I knelt next to it to peek inside. Did this one have an ID? She did. Davina Kellog, twenty-eight from Ardmore, Ok.

"She's a long way from home," I said.

I passed the identification to Jacoby and moved a few more things around.

"Look at this."

There was a card from that same transportation company.

"Let's get back to the office," Jacoby said. "We've seen enough here. We have got to figure out how to find this Travis."

"I agree," I responded as I stood. "But we still need to speak with the homeless guy."

"Anything to get me away from here." Jacoby walked away. But I couldn't move just yet. There was something holding me in place. There was something familiar about this place or at least reminiscent of some place I knew. What eluded me? There was something. Slowly, I backed away then turned on my heels to join Jacoby.

I made my way toward the street. They were just on the other side, shielded by a patrol car. I could hear the old homeless man speaking as I approached.

"Yeah, I saw him."

"Can you describe him?"

"He ain't look like you."

"What do you mean, not like me?" Jacoby questioned.

"Like him," he said as I rounded the vehicle.

"You mean he was Black?" Jacoby asked.

"He looked like him. 'Cept he had things in his head."

"What things?"

Instead of interjecting, I took note of his demeanor. It looked like it'd been a while since he'd showered. And it certainly smelled like it, the stale smell of urine wafted by me standing at least two feet from him. His shoes were worn, dirt layered his clothes. His jacket was army green. He was a bit jittery. His head constantly in motion. All the signs of someone paranoid or on drugs or both.

"You know."

He moved his hand from the top of his head and then motioned to his shoulder.

"Dreadlocs?" I asked.

"Yeah, yeah, that's them."

"What else can you tell me about him?" Jacoby asked.

"I'on know man!"

"Come on, Jake. What can you tell me?"

"I done told you. He looked like him." He pointed at me without looking in my direction.

"Do you know what he was driving?"

"It was black."

"Like a car, truck, van?"

"That," he said at Jacoby's last word.

"A van?"

"Yeah."

"Ok."

"Jacoby." I motioned for him to come my way.

"What's up?"

"I have an idea. How 'bout we put him up in a motel? Get him cleaned up, some food, and a comfortable place to sleep. If he's a bit more relaxed, maybe we can get some straight answers."

Jacoby nodded, then went back to speak with Jake. Everything about Jake's behavior screamed PTSD to me. Getting him comfortable, relaxed, and feeling safe might help him open up. But more than that, we couldn't let him out of our sight. He was a witness that we needed to protect at all costs.

I instructed Officer Washington where to take Jake, and to stand guard outside until we sent him relief. Jake would have around the clock protection.

The excitement was all over Jacoby's face once we made it back to the car.

"This might be just the break we're looking for."

"It may." I had my cell phone to my ear. "Robin, we need a background on Jake Peters. Yeah. Ok. We're headed back now."

"Oh, Jake is the best thing to happen to us."

While Jacoby was optimistic, I wasn't so much. Jake could be making all this up. Not that I didn't believe he saw what he said he saw, but his mind might not be all that reliable. I wanted to, but putting all my eggs in that basket didn't seem all that safe.

"Hopefully."

"Come on, Barton. Have just a little optimism."

"I'm trying, really trying."

My voice trailed off as I looked out the window. My mind went with it.

"It looks like the Gemini Killer strikes again. There has been another incident involving a discovered body of a young woman. Sources close to the police department are saying that she was found hanging by her neck."

"Who the fuck's feeding them this shit?" the chief yelled as he shut off the television in the station. "They gave this guy a name. Our phone lines haven't stopped ringing."

No one in the squad room said a thing; many looked around as if they were waiting for someone else to speak up. I stood leaning against the wall at the back. I wanted to know who was leaking information, probably more than he did.

I didn't listen to anything else the chief had to say. He was more focused on the number of phone calls the tipline was getting than actually finding the killer. I halfway think he didn't want the killer to be caught for a few reasons. One being that this Black detective would be proven to out police him. That glory wouldn't be credited to him. All he was worried about was his reputation.

It wasn't until Jacoby got in front of the room that I tuned back in.

"We have a loose description of a person of interest. We are not releasing this information to the public at this time. The information we have is too vague. The last thing we need or want is a lynch mob on our hands."

There was grumbling through the room. He used those words intentionally.

"The subject is believed to be a Black man with dreadlocks, possibly in a black van. Those are all the details we have."

"What can we do with that?" someone in the room called out.

"Be mindful. This is not carte blanche to harass any Black man you see. There's enough of that. Just be mindful. Until we get more definitive, confirmed executable information, we cannot go kicking in doors or taking names. Tensions are high enough now that the press is involved. We need you to pay close attention to any abandoned or broken-down vehicles. I implore you to check out any vehicles on the side of the road. And by all means, get assistance for any women in need."

He gave them some encouragement, and then everyone was on their way. I watched them file out, listening to the grumbling as they walked by. Nothing like this had ever happened in this town. Most of these officers never imagined having to deal with this kind of crime. And half, if not more, didn't really care because the victims were a skin tone not of their own.

"Boss," Robin called for my attention. "Call for you."

I made my way to my desk to retrieve the call.

"Barton."

"Hi, Detective Barton. This is Mrs. Elkins

"Yes. How may I help you today?"

"First, I want to apologize for what I said."

"No apology needed."

"I'm calling about the support group."

"Support group?"

"Yeah, Crystal was going to this support group over at that church over on Hampstead and Cannon, I think. I can't think of its name."

"Thank you so much. That is very helpful."

"I hope you find who did this."

"We will. And I'll let you know when we find anything."

"Thank you, Detective."

"God bless you, Mrs. Elkins

"We got action!" I yelled to Jacoby.

Chapter 10

MOUNT CARMEL MISSIONARY BAPTIST Church had the look of a schoolhouse. You could tell at first sight, it'd been there a while. There were more cars in the parking lot than we expected on a Wednesday afternoon. A lot more.

The car had barely rolled to a stop before I was opening the passenger door. I'd taken to letting Jacoby drive; there was something about the aesthetics of me driving him that didn't sit quite right with me.

It didn't seem that anyone milling around the church paid too much attention to us as we strolled toward the doors. The closer we got to the building the more we could digest what was happening. Looks like we arrived in the middle of their food drive.

Instead of approaching, we stood off to the side observing and assessing the patrons and leaders. I'd spotted the pastor right away. He was the one with a glowing smile, shaking hands with everyone who made their way near him.

From where I stood, I estimated him to be about 5'7", between 200–225 lb. His shade is a bit darker than mine, and his face is close-shaven, with a short fade.

It seemed the women had a little sparkle in their eyes when they were near him. I wondered if he was *that* kind of pastor, if he was single or married. Whether he 'laid hands' on his parishioners. The notion of that made me think about my parents. They had me in Bible study every Thursday evening. Vacation Bible school every summer. And we were all in the front pew every Sunday.

That was...until it came out that Pastor Proctor had fathered a child with Sister Mason. And that might have been excusable if Sister Mason wasn't twenty years his junior and married to Deacon Oliver. My mom seemed to take it especially hard. I remember her crying her eyes out. And I also recalled the argument with my father afterward.

"Ready?"

Jacoby pulled me back from the memory as he began walking toward the good pastor. I followed.

"Good afternoon, I'm Pastor Whitlock. What brings you here, officers?"

"What makes you think we're law enforcement?" Jacoby questioned, with a smile.

"Well, sir. I wasn't always a pastor."

They shared a laugh, but I didn't.

He was one of *those* types of pastors. The one from the streets that turned his life around. The kind that couldn't shake that aura of 'hustler' around him. Full of charm, charisma, and confidence.

"What can I do for you fellows?"

"I'm Agent Jacoby, this is Detective Barton. We wanted to chat with you about your support group."

"Which one? We have several initiatives going on."

"It would've been one involving pregnant women," I chimed in.

"We have a woman's support group and an expectant mother support group. Sister Candice runs both. She's probably the one you need to speak to. May I ask who you're inquiring about?"

"Crystal Elkins, are you familiar?" I asked.

"I can't say that I am. There's Sister Candice over there." He nodded in her direction. "I'm sure she'll be able to answer any of your questions."

"Thank you, Pastor," Jacoby said.

I nodded his way, then we both headed in the direction of Sister Candice.

Sister Candice was pointing at a few young men telling them to help this patron or another carry their things. Her back was to us when we got close to her.

"Are you Sister Candice?"

"Who's asking?" she said as she turned around to face us.

When she looked at me, she smiled, then her facial expression changed.

"I'm Agent Jacoby, this is Detective Barton. We wanted to ask you some questions about Crystal Elkins."

"Crystal? What done happened? Did those babies come already? When she didn't come last week I figured them babies was giving her a run for her money. Is everything alright?"

"I'm sorry to inform you, but Crystal is no longer with us."

The particulars were left out. We were here to gather information, not give it.

"Oh Jesus." She closed her eyes, saying a short prayer. "What happened?"

"That's what we're trying to find out, ma'am."

"When's the last time you saw Crystal?" I inquired.

"It was a few weeks ago."

"Do you know if she was having any trouble with anyone?" Jacoby questioned.

"No. Crystal was the sweetest. She would sometimes stay after to help me clean up."

"I've been told Crystal had trouble with drugs," I informed.

"We all have something we're not proud of. She would never hurt those babies."

"Sometimes we leave things alone, and it doesn't want to leave us alone. Was there anyone from her past who may not have been happy with her, or did she owe money?"

Sister Candice shook her head.

"No one that I know of," she replied.

"What about a boyfriend?" Jacoby questioned.

Sister Candice shook her head.

"And the children's father?" Jacoby asked.

"She never told me who it was."

"Was there anyone in the group she was especially close to?"

"No one I know of. What about the babies?"

I took a deep breath. Then Jacoby jumped in to answer.

"Fortunately, one of them is thriving. Unfortunately, there is currently a search for the other."

Her mouth dropped open and her eyes doubled in size.

"You mean to tell me, she was one of the ones you talked about on the news."

We didn't say anything. Tears filled her eyes.

"If you think of anything else, please give me a call." I handed her my card.

"Thank you," Jacoby said.

We made our way back to the car.

Sister Candice asking about the kids took me to a place I didn't want to be. In my head.

Just before Jacoby was about to pull off, Sister Candice appeared at the passenger door. I let the window down.

"There is one thing I thought about, Crystal talking about this guy."

She handed me a business card. The same business card for Travis Moore.

"Have you seen this person?"

"No. I haven't. A conversation we had just popped into my head. She made a point to put the card in her purse, just in case something went wrong with her car. I don't know if she ever needed to use it or not. But just in case."

"Thank you."

"We have GOT to find Travis Moore," Jacoby said before pulling out of the parking lot.

I was sitting in the situation room staring at all the information we had, just hoping something I hadn't seen before would jump out at me. Robin was working on tracking down Travis Moore. He was moving further up the list of people of interest. Shit, he was the only person of interest.

My focus was on the photos from the last crime scene. There was something about the entire display that kept gnawing at me. Maybe it was because it was fresh in my mind. The eeriness of the location still lingered. There was something familiar about it. My phone chimed just as Robin walked in.

"Boss, still trying to narrow down Travis Moore."

"Give me whatever history you can on this place."

I pointed at the abandoned childcare center where our last victim was found.

"You got it."

My phone rang.

"Hey, babe."

"Are you going to be home for dinner today?"

"I think I can make that happen for you."

"Good."

"I shouldn't be here too much longer."

"That's what I wanted to hear. I'd much rather have you as my security than Officer Cameron."

"I know you don't like it, but better safe than sorry."

"I know."

She was trying not to sound worried for my sake. But I knew her, her tones, her pitches and the way she thought. My wife was afraid and I hated it. I would have given anything to be able to go home, sit with my wife and be her protection twenty-four seven. But I knew the best way to protect her would be to take this player off the board.

"How about I give you a nice foot rub when I get home?"

"That sounds nice."

"Be naked."

"Now you're talking my language."

We disconnected. That's when I remembered to check the notification that had come in just before Robin came in. I had a text message from an unlisted number. As soon as I opened the message, I jumped up from my seat.

"Robin!" I yelled.

She scrambled across the squad room, into our situation room.

"What's up, Boss?"

I wasn't even sure what to say, where to start. I stared at my phone. Robin could tell by the look on my face something was very wrong. She approached me cautiously.

"What's going on, Boss?"

"He sent me a message," I responded, handing her my phone.

When she saw what was on my phone's screen, she gasped and instantly tears formed in her eyes.

"I'll get the tech guys on this right away."

She turned on her heels and headed out of the room. That's when I cleared my thoughts, then refocused on the phone. I needed to find some clue in the photo I'd been sent. There on my phone was a picture of one of the missing children. The good thing was, it, because I couldn't tell the sex, was alive.

Waiting to be saved.

There were people scampering around in the squad room, I couldn't take my eyes off my cell phone. Questions, statements, more questions swam in my head. Jacoby, coming to the door broke the trance.

"What does it say?"

Assuming Robin filled him in, I handed him my phone then plopped into my seat as I stared at nothing.

"What does this mean?" he asked.

I shrugged.

"Why is he sending this to you? How did he get your number?"

These were questions I had as well, but the answers I didn't.

"He's taunting us, you. This puts a new spin on all this."

"I know," I said absently.

"We need more bodies, more brains."

"Not any of them," I said as I pointed toward the larger room.

"I'm calling in a special profiler."

Jacoby pulled out his cell phone. On the other hand, I was still in my head. *What the fuck is going on?* Then something hit me. I turned to my desk phone and dialed Serita.

"Hey, babe. What's going on?"

When she picked up, I had to remind myself to watch my tone.

"Just checking on you. How are you feeling today?"

"I'm fine."

I could tell by the drag in her voice that she was suspicious. We'd just talked.

"Something came up, it's going to be a late night."

"Thanks for letting me know. Was there a break in the case?" I didn't respond. "You'll get answers soon, babe."

I smiled. Here she was trying to lift my spirits.

"Your vote of confidence means a lot. Don't be over there doing too much."

"Oh, I'm not. Officer Cameron might as well do something other than sit outside. I put him to work."

I chuckled. That sounded like something I should've expected.

"I love you, woman. See you later."

"See you."

After placing the handset in the cradle, I looked up at an awaiting Jacoby.

"Help is on the way."

My right brow rose, asking a question without speaking.

"The bureau is sending us the best profiler I've seen in years."

"Who?"

"Shania Brindle."

Chapter 11

"How long am I going to need an escort?" Serita questioned as I picked up my coffee mug from the counter.

"As long as there's a serial killer running around Lawton."

"Two days ago, I didn't even need to know about it. Now, it's top-flight security."

She tried to laugh it off. But I knew she was trying to divert her nervousness. I couldn't blame her, and no way would I show mine.

"Better safe, right?"

"Yeah," she said lowly.

"What's on your agenda today?"

"Just a little baby shopping. And I have a doctor's appointment."

"Do I need to be there?"

"Of course not. You need to be catching killers."

"Babe, please try not to worry."

"Easier said than done."

"That's why I got you a watchdog."

"Whatever," she said, rolling her eyes dramatically.

Placing my cup back on the counter then wrapping my arms around her, I kissed her forehead. Something I always did when I wanted to reassure her.

"We're gonna catch him, and our world will get back to its normal self."

"Your mouth to God's ears."

I kissed her lips. "My word is what matters."

She leaned into the kiss. "Get out of here and get to catching."

"Sources tell us, the Gemini Killer has contacted the Lawton police department. It has been an intense night for detectives and the FBI. We do not have the details as of yet. WHBN would just like to remind everyone to be safe. There are currently four amber alerts in effect."

"Who the FUCK is talking to the press?" Jacoby stood at the front of the squad room, not mincing words.

"When we find you, we will find you; that will be your last day here!" Saronson chimed in.

I scanned the room to see their reactions.

"It was that one there."

I could see a finger pointing over my shoulder, but didn't know who it belonged to. The voice next to me was unfamiliar so was the face when I turned to look. This woman was mid-twenties, maybe early thirties. She wore dreadlocks, mocha skin and donned a face that said, she was about her business.

"How can you say that?"

My question wasn't because I doubted what she said; I'd come to the same conclusion. I needed to see her reasoning.

"You saw them shift. Totally opposite of what everyone else did. It was him. We just have to prove it."

Whatever else Saronson or Jacoby said, I'd tuned out.

"How do we do that?"

"Feed him some information that is either unknown or false and see where it goes."

"Like, we have the name of the person one of the victims was last seen with?"

"Exactly!"

I nodded while I pushed myself off the wall.

"Barton," I said, extending my hand.

"Brindle."

"Nice to meet you, I've heard great things."

"Ditto."

Everyone in the room began moving, signifying that this debrief was over. Jacoby made his way to us.

"Shania, thanks for coming."

"Where else would I be?"

"I'm sure there are plenty of cases that could use your expertise."

"But none quite like this one. Plus, how could I put anything over missing babies?"

I didn't know if their banter was jovial or serious. What I did know was that, as far as I had seen, Ms. Brindle would live up to her reputation.

"I'll be right back."

I headed in Macon's direction to feed him the false information. We'd see if it made the evening or morning news.

"Tell me the part you're leaving out."

Shania Brindle wasn't at all what I expected. Younger than I'd assumed. She was guarded but tried not to appear so. And seeing her made me wonder how many women profilers the FBI employed. Then I wondered how many were Black.

Shania was indeed sharper than the average knife. She'd joined us in the situation room, Jacoby briefed her on the details, speculations and the next steps we'd planned. She had gone over all the notes posted, photos displayed. We'd filled her in on the photo I'd received of one of the children and the message. Everything we knew about the case, she knew but somehow, she knew there was still something left out.

Jacoby looked in my direction as if I were on stage and he was waiting for me to perform. Shania stood in the middle of the floor looking between both of us waiting for an answer.

I leaned against the desk, took a deep breath, and then spoke.

"My wife is pregnant. With twins."

The expression on her face didn't change. But I felt like I could see the gears in her head churning.

"Before the photo, had he contacted you?"

"No..." I paused. "At least not that I can prove."

"What do you mean?" Jacoby asked.

"There have been a few calls directed to my desk that were hang-ups. I had Robin trace them, but there was nothing definitive."

The room was silent for some minutes.

"Ok. Can you think of anyone in your past who would be capable of this?"

"You mean career-wise? Hell no. This is Lawton."

"What about personally?"

I shook my head. "It's just me and my wife."

"Disgruntled ex?"

My shaking head was my answer.

"Family?"

"My parents died when I was eighteen."

"Siblings?"

"I was adopted. It was just me. My parents didn't have any other kids."

"Other relatives?"

"My parents had other relatives."

"Could this be any of them?"

I gave her notion just a second of thought. "Naw."

"So. Why you?"

"I've been asking the same question. The only answer I came up with was Serita."

"The pregnant wife."

"Yup."

"Which takes us back to this imaging center," she stated.

"Yup."

She stood and walked closer to the whiteboard. She took the business card of the transportation service.

"We can't find his name registered anywhere. I know there must be some kind of connection, but we can't draw the line."

Shania picked up one of the markers and began writing letters. She rearranged the letters of Travis's name. Then again under that arrangement of letters then again under that then again. Then again, until.

"What about this name?"

She stepped back as she underlined the last of the letters, drawing a line under them.

Rosie V. Marto

My heart dropped. My face must've done something, too. I know I felt like all the blood drained from it.

"What?" Jacoby questioned.

"Do you know that name?" Shania asked.

I nodded. They looked at me expectantly. There was so much hesitation in what came next.

"That's the name of my birth mother."

Chapter 12

I WOKE UP THE next morning on the couch with a cramp in my neck. Shania had me at the station until the wee hours of the morning, going through my life. She wanted to know everything I knew about my birth mother, which wasn't much. I could only tell her what I'd been told as a child. Which was simply that my mother couldn't care for me, so she gave me to my adoptive parents to raise. She wanted me to have a better life than she did.

I couldn't fill in any other blanks, and my parents' family didn't really fuck with me. I hadn't spoken to any of them since my parents died. I was never told who my birth father was. And of course, I'd looked up my birth mother years ago. According to what I knew, she died shortly after I was given up. Drug overdose. Shania had rounds of questions, and I answered what I could.

But by the time we were done it was so late, there was no way I was going up to wake Serita when I got in. So, the couch it was. I stretched out then looked at my watch wondering what time it was. I didn't smell any coffee so it must've still been early. But the sun was out. When I looked at the time I sat straight up. I was going to be late. It was already nearly 7:30.

Serita was usually up by this time with coffee on for me. My first thought was that she was mad at me for not coming home. Then a jolt of fear hit me. I bounded up the stairs to our bedroom, nearly knocking the door from the hinges.

"What the fuck?" Serita hollered with wide eyes.

I dropped to my knees at the foot of the bed. With my head resting on the comforter, I willed my eyes to dry. I didn't want to scare her any more than we both were already. She tried to shield me from her fear, but I knew she was terrified.

"Thank GOD!"

"What is wrong with you?"

"Nothing," I said into the comforter.

"Don't tell me, 'nothing'. You came barreling in here because of something."

"I'm just on edge. This case."

"You thought somebody snatched me because you didn't smell coffee, didn't you?"

Chuckling, I lifted my head to look at her.

"Yeah."

Her expression softened.

One of the pros and cons of your wife knowing you so well. She could practically read my mind, all the time.

"What's going on with the case?"

I gave her a look, but before I could say anything, she continued, "Don't give me that shit about leaving work at work. We agreed you would let me know what was going on with this case."

"You're right," I conceded. "The suspect seems to be communicating with me."

"What? How?"

"He sent me a photo of one of the missing babies."

She took in a sharp breath.

"The baby was alive," I said.

Then I could visibly see her exhaling.

"Thank God."

"There's something else. This new profiler came in."

"Oh yeah."

"It's a Black woman."

"That's dope."

"Young Black woman. I'm guessing she's in her late twenties or early thirties."

"Impressive."

"Very."

"And how did that go?"

"Well...good and bad."

"What's the good?"

"She may have found a new lead."

"That's not good, it's fantastic. What could be bad about that?"

"It seems like this killer may somehow have a connection to me."

"How?"

I explained to her how we got to my birth mother's name, and because of that, I was being questioned into the early morning. Her face was full of worry.

"Officer Cameron will be here at nine. He'll escort you anywhere you need to go. Please try not to worry."

"I know you got me covered. What about the kids?"

"We're doing all we can to find them."

"The news stations have given him a name."

"I know. The Gemini Killer."

"It's awful."

"This new lead brings us closer to catching this guy."

"Be safe," she said while reaching for my hand.

I got up from my knee and then rounded the bed. Leaning over, I planted a kiss on her lips.

"This will be over soon. I promise."

"Don't do that. Don't promise things you can't control. I know you'll do your best."

There wasn't really much I could say to that. She was right, I couldn't guarantee anything at this point. I could hope, but there was no guarantee.

"I gotta get dressed, I'm going to be late. Wait. Are you ok? What's got you in bed so late?"

"These two jokers in my belly. They were in there fighting last night, I swear. Maybe they were waiting up for you like I tried to."

She laughed, then moved as if she were getting out of bed.

"No. You get some rest. I don't need you to make me coffee. I'll get some at the office. Officer Cameron should be here by nine."

"I might not go back to sleep, but I sure will lie here for a little bit."

As she lay back, I got up from the bed and headed to the bathroom.

Serita turned on the television while I was in the shower. The newscast played as I dressed.

"It is another day without answers for the FBI and Lawton law enforcement. Sources tell us they are no closer to the Gemini Killer. There are still active amber alerts for the children. The only details we have about the children are that they are all African American newborns. It is unclear as to the sex of the children. It appears they were taken at birth. We are here to remind you to be cautious. WKPJ will continue to give updates as they come in."

"Sources!" I said with a bit of indignation.

"They didn't say anything about the new lead," she pointed out.

"That's because the only people who know about it are me, Jacoby, Robin, and Shania. We are keeping things close to our chests, seeing as how the news has 'Sources'."

"Makes sense."

After I dressed, I made my way over to Serita to plant another kiss on her lips.

"What do you have planned for the day?"

She shrugged. "I may go out to do a little baby shopping."

"Don't go anywhere without Cameron."

"I won't."

Chapter 13

WHEN I ARRIVED AT the station it was buzzing a bit more than usual. Especially at this early hour.

"What's up?"

Shania had beaten me in. She was sitting with her back to me, staring at the board we'd created in our make-shift office.

"Apparently, there were several calls to 9-1-1 about seeing a man snatch a lady somewhere around here."

"Where? What type of vehicle? How long ago? Why didn't anyone call me?"

"Because that's not our guy."

"How do you know?"

She turned around to face me.

"Because he isn't sloppy. There's no way multiple people saw him snatch anyone."

"Maybe he's getting desperate. Like with the local women."

"Still didn't have any witnesses."

"Well, there was the old homeless guy."

"One guy. Speaking of which, I want to talk to him."

I nodded.

"But first, more questions for you."

"I can't tell you anything else about my birth mother than I already have."

She shook her head.

"Not about your mother. And I guess it's more observations than questions. Just some things I wonder if you've considered."

"Shoot."

"You would agree that you're connected to this case in some way, right? Outside of the fact that our main suspect's name is an anagram of your birth mother, you're the only one he's contacted. You said you had a few hang-ups. We can't confirm that it was him, but it's highly likely. And we for sure know the photo sent to you was from him."

I simply nodded.

"There's a very high probability that he's been watching you for some time."

Again, I nodded. I wanted to see where she was going.

"Can you think of anyone that you wronged in some way?"

"No."

"What about seeing anyone suspicious lurking around? And not recently but ever."

After taking a beat to really think about it, I came up with nothing.

"Not off the top of my head. But that's one of those things that'll linger in the back of my mind. Something might come to me later."

"Understandable. I did try to talk to your adoptive extended family and got nowhere."

"Told ya!"

"I got the sense that they know more but won't say."

To that, I shrugged. Because what could I do about it? But then I had a thought.

"You think if you paid a visit to them in person, they'd talk? Maybe flashing a badge and looking in someone's face other than mine would loosen their lips or jog a memory."

"Perhaps. I have something else in the works, if that doesn't pan out then I may just have to do that."

"What's that?"

She hesitated.

"I'd rather not say just yet. *But* if it pans out like I'm hoping, we may have a few more answers this afternoon."

"So, the old vet. We can go pull up on him."

As we rode to the motel we had him put up in, I tried to garner a little more insight on Shania Brindle. It was obvious she was bright. Even before she figured out my birth mother's name. But there was something off about her. I couldn't quite put my finger on it, but it was something.

"So, where do you call home?"

"I'm on the road so much, sometimes I forget I have one."

We laughed. She continued, "I pay rent in Chicago."

"Any family in Chicago?"

She shook her head. "It's just me."

"You're an orphan like me," I stated with a chuckle.

"Not exactly. My mom was killed when I was young, and my father went missing a few years ago."

"I'm sorry."

"It's cool. You didn't know."

"Is that why you became a profiler?"

"Initially, I began studying criminal justice because of what happened to my mom. I had always been an inquisitive kid. Then I discovered I had a knack for being able to see how other people think. My dad was ex-military, so he taught me a lot of defensive and survival skills, all that, spiraled into this."

She waved her hands between the two of us.

"We're here," I said, pulling up in front of the motel.

"That was fast."

"Lawton, Oklahoma, is not that big."

We both climbed out, I headed to room 130, and Shania followed. He hadn't answered the door. Ten minutes later, I was standing in front of the clerk.

"Did you see when 130 left?"

"I didn't see him leave," the clerk responded.

"Give me the key."

Once we let ourselves into the room, we could tell that he'd taken the few things he had.

"Fuck!"

"You didn't have anyone sitting on him?"

Shania got a side-eye as opposed to the sarcastic shit I wanted to say.

"Chief wouldn't spring for a detail."

"He's a piece of work."

"Understatement."

I looked around the empty room, disgusted.

"Well, let's try driving by where you found him."

"Good idea."

We rode nearly an hour with no luck. I even stopped at a couple of shelters to see if he was there. It didn't make sense to me that he would leave a motel to go to a shelter but you never know.

"We might as well head back. Maybe he'll show back up at the motel."

"Maybe."

As soon as we arrived at the station, Shania's phone chimed. She looked at it and began smiling.

"That information came through. Let's get this laptop up and maybe find some answers."

"Go ahead. I'm going to call the motel and let them know to call us if he shows up. Then check in with my wife. I'll be up in a minute."

As I walked through the door of our office, Shania's and Jacoby's heads shot up.

"What's up?" I asked.

They were looking like...well, I can't describe what they looked like. There was something written on their faces and I needed them to tell me what it was.

"That information I was waiting on," she paused, looking at Jacoby.

"Yeah," I egged her on.

"Your sealed adoption papers."

I rushed over to the desk where she and Jacoby hovered over the laptop.

"What? How? What does it say?"

They both stepped back as I read over what was on the screen.

"This...this...isn't saying what I think it is. I...I...don't understand."

"How about you take a seat," Jacoby said.

Absentmindedly, I sat. Not that sitting would make me digest anything I'd just read any better or at all. My eyes were still on the screen, but I was no longer reading. The words, letters, and everything were just a blur. Shania was the first to speak.

"According to this, your mother gave you to the Masons and kept your brother."

"My twin!"

Neither of them had a rebuttal for that.

"This doesn't make sense."

Pulling my phone out of my pocket, I dialed Serita again. She still didn't answer. After dialing her again immediately and getting no answer, I decided to call Cameron.

"What's up, Boss?" he answered.

"Where are you at?"

"What do you mean? I'm grabbing something to eat like you told me."

"Like I told you?"

My voice was laced with confusion.

"Are you ok, Boss?"

"Cameron, I never told you to get food."

"Boss, you said to grab something to eat right after I told you I like your haircut."

"WHERE ARE YOU?" I yelled as I jumped up from my seat.

"I'm just over at the food court. Boss, I'll come right back over."

"Cameron, that wasn't me. I haven't cut my hair."

I began moving; Jacoby and Shania were on my heels. I jumped into my car without waiting for either of them. Shania made it into the passenger seat while Jacoby had to jump in his own ride.

"Boss, I'm back over at the store. She's gone."

"Fuck!"

I threw the phone down as I sped through traffic headed to the only place they could have been in this small town. Shania had picked up the radio and began talking. I didn't hear a word she said.

The car came to a screeching halt in front of the mall's double doors. I'd driven right on the walkway, blocking the entrance. Whether I even put the car in park is a question I don't know the answer to, but I was out of the car and running through the mall in seconds.

"Serita!"

"Serita!"

I ran through the mall screaming her name.

Did it make sense? No. Was she likely in the mall? No. Was I out of my mind? Yes. I dropped to my knees in the center of the mall.

"Serita!"

"Boss," Cameron said softly.

When I looked up at his face, his remorse was evident.

"What happened?"

"He looked just like you. He sounded like you. Came right up to me, called me by name. I even remarked that you'd cut your hair. I'm sorry, Boss. I thought it was you."

By this time, Shania and Jacoby were standing right beside him. I looked at each of them in the face, then stood. Shania handed me my cell phone; I guess she'd grabbed it from the car.

"Call her," she said.

The look I gave her said don't be ridiculous, but I did it anyway. Just as it began to ring on my end, a chime echoed through the open space. One of the uniforms that had arrived yelled.

"Over here."

He pointed to a trash can. I shook my head. Cameron looked at me with tears in his eyes. I wanted to give him some words of solace, reassurance, comfort, but I couldn't muster any.

Shania started questioning Cameron about any other details she could. I heard Jacoby ordering someone to the security office to review the video surveillance. But I checked out. I began walking to the entrance my car was blocking.

"Where are you going?" Jacoby called after me.

"Home."

Chapter 14

WHEN I PULLED IN the driveway, I looked around to see if anything looked suspicious. On the ride over, I began to wonder if he'd be here waiting for me with her. *Had he set a trap?* Nothing looked out of the ordinary. But would it?

Entering the house cautiously, I called out for Serita. Silence. I went through the motions of clearing the house, gun drawn. No one was here or had been here.

Feeling defeated, I plopped down on the sofa. My head dropped to the back, and the tears rolled into my ears. What was I going to do without her? Why did he take her? What did he want from me? Hell, where has he been all my life?

My ringing phone jolted me out of the pity party I was having. It also made my heart leap. What if it were him? Immediately, I scrambled to dig the phone out of my pants pocket. I let out an exasperated breath when I saw the chief's name flash across my screen.

I didn't have the energy to deal with him so I silenced it. It rang again; I didn't look at it. It rang again; I snatched it up.

"Yeah?"

"I know this isn't the best time. We've got to talk all this through," Shania said.

"I can't right now."

"You're going to have to. We're on our way over."

I just ended the call. I didn't even have the energy to oppose her. My phone chirped. It wasn't my regular text notification. Cautiously, I looked at my phone screen, I sat straight up, and opened the app.

"I'm coming, baby," I said aloud as I headed out the door.

It had been at least fifteen minutes of me barreling down the highway before my phone rang.

"Yeah?"

"Barton, where are you? I told you we were on our way."

"I know where she is."

"What? How? Did he contact you? It's probably a trap."

"No. Her ear pods. He may have thrown her phone in the trash, but her earbuds are always in her pocket. She set up that thing where we could find them because she was always leaving them. My phone pinged with some ad that reminded me. I'm going to get my wife."

"Send us the address. I'm calling for backup. Wait for backup."

Even though she knew when it came out of her mouth, I wasn't waiting. I didn't bother to say it. I didn't say anything; I hung up. I sent her the address but I was now ten minutes away. Which meant they were at least twenty-five minutes behind me. No way was I waiting.

It was in view. A dilapidated farmhouse sat by itself at least twenty feet from the dirt road. The logical thing would've been to wait. But the area was wide open, there was no way he wouldn't see us coming if he were looking. I had a split second to decide whether I was going to let him hear me coming or try sneaking up on him.

The former was faster; the longer I took, the closer to harm she could be.

Turning my car onto the long drive that led to the farmhouse, I floored it. It wasn't until I came to a full stop in front of the house that I noticed the pole barn behind it. If there was any killing going on, that's where I'd do it.

I climbed out of my car, closing the door quietly.

Maybe he hadn't heard me pull in.

My service weapon was drawn as I approached the farmhouse. Moving slowly around it, I peered into the windows. There was no movement, no one in sight. I continued cautiously toward the back of the house. I paused at the back corner, looking toward the pole barn that was about another ten to fifteen feet away. To the left was a chicken coop, and a pig pen was just on the other side of that.

There were no windows in the barn. And its doors were closed. So, I ran for it.

Gingerly, I stepped around the barn to see if there were any other ways in. Nope, just those front doors.

The entire time, I was listening intently. There was a male voice I could hear faintly. I couldn't make out what he was saying. Making my way to the barn doors, I was running my next movements through my head. I needed to swing the doors open and keep my gun up. How the fuck was I going to do that? I needed to draw him out.

I ran over to the pig pen, unlatched the gate then slapped one of the pigs. It squealed and took off. The other quickly followed. Then I dashed back to the side of the barn. The pigs were squealing but I wasn't sure that would be enough to get him out. *Can he hear them?*

Then I bumped the side of the barn. But I made my way back to come around on the other side. When he came out to investigate, he'd see the pigs. That should prompt him to wrangle them back into the pen. I'd slip in, get Serita, then handle him. That's the way I planned it anyway.

Crouched down, I waited. Then I realized the cavalry would be pulling up at any minute. I was running out of time. As soon as they came, this was going to be a hostage situation. He could hunker down in that barn. I was growing more anxious by the second.

Just when I was trying to think of something else to do, there was movement. The barn door creaked. I held my breath, willing him to do just what I had engineered.

"Grace! You done opened that gate again." I heard him say.

He'd taken a few steps.

"Come on, get in there."

I stood to my full height. In this grand plan, I hadn't factored in that there was no way he wouldn't see me go into the barn. But I had the gun. I took one step from the side of the barn, gun raised, and his back was turned to me. That's just what I needed. Quickly, I slipped into the ajar barn door.

There wasn't much light, just the sun coming through the cracks. Hay bales were lining the sides.

"Serita," I whispered.

I walked further into the barn, and I could see her at the back, slumped against a post in the back stall. Running to her, I was so relieved. Then I heard sirens in the distance. When I reached her, I dropped to my knees.

"Baby, I got you, we gotta get out of here."

She didn't respond.

"Baby."

I shook her shoulders, and her head flopped to one side. That's when I noticed blood on my hands. Crawling backward, then jumping to my feet, I could now see that the hay around her was red. It was soaked in blood, but I couldn't tell where it was coming from.

"Baby!"

"You're too late!"

Spinning around, I saw his face...then...

POW!

About the Author

KAYLYNN HUNT IS A multi-genre
author, screenwriter, and creative
visionary with a passion for telling
stories that blend real-life experiences
with imagination, grit, and heart.
Known for her bold voice and
emotionally rich narratives, Kaylynn
writes fiction that spans romance,
suspense, and drama—always centering
complex characters and powerful themes.

She is the founder of Skylar Publications LLC, an independent
publishing company dedicated to amplifying diverse voices and
creating generational wealth through storytelling. With a background
as an electrician, Kaylynn brings the same dedication and precision
to her creative work, often drawing inspiration from the everyday
strength of women and the resilience of the human spirit.

In addition to her books, Kaylynn is adapting several of her works into screenplays, including The Killing Path (Based from Hwy 725), and is actively building a production pipeline to bring these stories to life on screen.

When she's not writing, Kaylynn is championing fellow indie authors, collaborating on anthologies, and connecting with readers through live events and online interactions.